COWGIRL FOR KEEPS

LACY WILLIAMS

PROLOGUE

"*I*'m sorry I'm late..."

The unexpected female voice preceded a willowy young woman attempting to sit in Anna Brown's lap. Barely.

"Excuse me—" Anna grunted beneath the unexpected weight.

The formica tabletop wobbled as the other woman realized her mistake, her knee bumping the table and nudging the coffee-shop booth back with a grating *screech*. The two full coffee cups wobbled precariously, but Anna's friend Melody reached out to steady them from her seat across the table.

When the slender woman stood up, Anna got a good look at her. Dark hair was pulled back in a tight French braid. She had blue eyes and a flash of freckles across her nose. Vague recognition flared.

"I'm so sorry," the woman mumbled.

"It's you!" Melody's expression showed her surprise.

Still standing beside their table, the newcomer's head had been swiveling as she looked around the interior of the coffee shop, but at Melody's words, she focused back on the pair in the booth.

"It's me," she said on an exhale.

Anna looked between the young woman and Melody. "It's...?"

"The gal I loaned a gallon of gas," Melody said.

"Lila Andrews," the newcomer said at the same time.

"That was you?" Two days ago, Anna had seen the bright red classic car—she couldn't say what kind—stopped along the side of the road with the hood up, but she'd been rushing to pick Mikey up from baseball practice and hadn't been able to stop.

Lila rubbed a spot on her forehead. Color rose high in her cheeks. "Yes, that was me, Anna Campbell."

At the slightly snarky remark, Anna remembered. They'd gone to elementary school together, until Lila had been shipped off to boarding school around eighth grade. Lila had been a grade younger.

"It's Anna Brown now." Saying her married name still made her thumb run over the bare spot on her ring finger. She'd taken off the wedding ring at the last anniversary she'd celebrated alone.

"Do you want to sit down?" Melody offered.

Lila took another glance around the coffee shop. Spring rains had pushed most folks off Main Street—not that Redbud Trails boasted much of a shopping hub—and more booths were filled than usual, but apparently, whomever she'd been running late to meet wasn't there, because she perched gingerly on Melody's side of the booth with a mumbled, "Thanks."

When Lila stretched her neck—again—Anna wrinkled her nose at Melody. This was their only time to grab coffee and have girl chat. Between Anna's responsibilities on the family ranch and her work corralling her two kids, time was tight. But Melody, who owned a dress-shop in town, had to have one of the softest hearts of anyone Anna knew, so it wasn't surprising she would invite Lila to sit.

"So you're back in town?" Anna asked.

"The prodigal returns. Or something like that." Lila's fingertips drummed on the tabletop. Nervous? "What does your husband do?"

Anna's throat closed up, but she soldiered on. "I'm a widow."

Something in Lila's demeanor softened. "I'm sorry."

So was Anna. It had been three years, but her grief remained.

"This is our weekly girl time," Melody said.

Lila's expression cooled. "I'm sorry to have interrupted."

She started scooting toward the edge of the booth, and something in the vicinity of Anna's heart twinged. Lila's nervousness, her admission that she was the prodigal coming home... maybe she needed a friend too.

"Wait," she said.

"Stay," Melody agreed.

Lila considered them, a grain of vulnerability visible

beneath her cool expression. "Okay. I guess you guys could use a friend like me."

A laugh bubbled out of Anna at the outrageous statement. A new friend.

A new start?

CHAPTER 1

"*M*o-om!"

"Gina's telling!"

Rolling her eyes even as she ignored the shouts of her children, Anna Brown kicked a soccer ball through the front hall and into the coat closet, where the mishmash of winter boots, baseball mitt and bat, child-sized lariat, and who knew what else wobbled precariously before she slammed the door shut.

Afternoon sunlight streamed through the skinny windows bracketing the front door, and she squinted against it as she kept moving. Feet pounded on the stairs. Dinner was barely over. Couldn't they wait five minutes before picking a fight with each other?

Her arms full of a pair of backpacks, a teddy bear, a stuffed dog toy, and two pairs of outgrown cowboy boots, she rushed through the living room and into the home office that had become the catch-all room. Her

5

gaze went to the barn, visible through the wide window. How she'd love an evening ride.

But reality intruded. Bills were piled on the desk, tall enough that they obscured the bottom part of the window. Gina's ballet gear was piled on the sofa. And on the wall, she carefully kept her gaze averted from the calendar with one upcoming date circled in red. Her birthday.

This room had become the heart of the house.

There was a time that honor had belonged to the kitchen—her favorite room of the house—but not for several months, since the contractor debacle.

But hopefully today would change that.

She dumped her armload on the sofa next to the door and whirled back to the hall, closing the door with a snap just in time to catch the two human whirlwinds that plowed into her.

"Oof!"

She put a hand on each of their shoulders and drew them apart.

"Mikey kicked me!"

"She punched me first—"

"Only because he stole my doll!"

"Guys!" She clapped her hands once, loudly, and they froze, their almost-identical blue eyes wide.

Three and a half year old Gina bounced on the balls of her feet.

"Do you need to go to the bathroom?"

Gina shook her head vigorously.

"What's going on?"

When they started talking over each other, she had to clap again. "Mikey first."

Words burst from the eight-year-old. "Gina wouldn't let me change the TV to my superhero show. Then she threw the remote behind the couch."

She waited out his quick-stepping ramble.

After a moment, he ducked his head. "And then she punched me, and I kicked her."

She hated using the TV as a babysitter, but she had company coming—right now!—and had allowed a half hour after their quickly-consumed supper so she could clean up.

It was important company. She'd finally broken down and asked for help. Her preacher said he knew someone who could manage her kitchen problem.

Just then, someone knocked at the front door.

The kids' heads swiveled, but before they could race down the hall, she rested her hands on their shoulders again.

The minister would have to wait.

She squatted between the kids. "What's the golden rule? Gina?"

Her daughter gave a very convincing set of puppy dog eyes as she answered, "Tweet others as you want to be tweeted."

Lip twitching with the smile she had to hold back, Anna nodded. Then she turned her attention to Mikey.

There came another knock at the door. She sighed. The minister or her childrens' obedience? There was never enough of her to go around. She thought wistfully of the horses in the barn and the ride that would never be. She *did* have to visit the barn later, but only to care for the animals.

Both children glanced toward the door again, but Anna went on stubbornly.

"Mikey, were you using the golden rule when you were fighting with your sister?"

"No." The eight-year-old's lower lip stuck out in a petulant frown.

"So what should you say?"

"I'm sorry," he grumbled.

"Sowwy," Gina echoed.

It wasn't a perfect apology, but it would have to do. "Okay."

The bell rang again, and this time both Gina and Mikey took off, their boots pounding against the wood floors and exacerbating Anna's headache.

She followed behind, just slow enough to come up behind as Mikey opened the door.

There stood Paul Brookstead, the preaching minister at her church. And slightly behind, a man she'd hoped never to see again.

Kelly Matthews.

What was he doing here? Her mind whirled with possibilities, but she couldn't make sense of his presence on her front step.

"Hi, Mr. Paul!" Mikey greeted. He registered the stranger. "Who're you?"

The words yanked her out of the shock that had held her immobile.

The caramel brown eyes had more lines around the corners than she remembered. It was her first thought, because his eyes registered that first inkling of a smile.

Then his lips lifted, spread, in a devastating grin, and her heart thumped once, hard. She clutched the door.

"I'm Gina! I'm three years old." Her little girl piped up before anyone else had spoken.

Anna registered Gina now dancing from foot to foot.

"Gina—"

"I gotta go!" Gina didn't even glance backward as she sprinted down the hallway, her gait lilting because she'd just had a growth spurt and, mostly, because she was three.

Anna wished she could follow her daughter. Disappear.

Only instead of running back, like she knew Gina would in a few minutes, she wanted to stay gone.

Blindsided.

What was Kelly doing here? Why was he with Paul? Was this some sort of trick?

"My name is Kelly," he said to Mikey, and his voice was the same smooth baritone she remembered from their college days.

Paul stepped back a little, allowing Kelly to step forward and shake Mikey's hand. The men were still standing on the stoop.

She was so flustered, she hadn't even invited them in.

She held the door open, the only invitation she could offer.

KELLY MATTHEWS STEPPED over the threshold, half his attention on Anna's son and the well-constructed, if dated, foyer. The other half was on the woman herself.

Anna hadn't changed much in the nine years since he'd seen her last. She'd filled out a little, now with a woman's curves more so than a teen's, but her copper-colored hair and those snapping green eyes were the same ones that haunted his dreams even now.

She wasn't happy to see him.

He'd skipped supper because of the tangled knot of hope and anticipation in his stomach. And now it seemed it was just as well, because the knot rose to his throat, threatening to choke him.

He'd known this would be difficult. There was a reason Anna was the last visit on his list. He hadn't exactly been jumping for joy to humiliate himself to the woman he'd once loved.

But he'd made a vow to go through with it, one that he couldn't break.

He still had a fifty-fifty shot of this visit ending on a positive note. Or so he told himself. If the ice blasting from Anna's eyes was any indication, it might be more of a ten percent chance.

"Kelly is a general contractor," Paul was saying.

Nice guy. Kelly had tooled into town Monday morning and found himself on his knees in the empty church sanctuary, desperate for wisdom about how to reach out to Anna. Paul had found him there, and they'd struck up a conversation. Kelly had been honest about his motivation for seeing Anna, and it had gotten him this far, into her living room.

Furniture filled the room, and the three adults stood in the center. Would she ask them to sit down?

"Paul said you've got some problems with your kitchen."

Anna's expression darkened, but before she could respond, there was a tug on his right pants pocket. He looked down at the tot who was a carbon-copy of her mother, except for those bright blue eyes. Those came from her father. She must've tiptoed up behind him, because he hadn't heard her return after running off before.

"Our kitchen is broke," the little girl said, her eyes wide and serious.

"Mom can't cook in there no more," Mikey said. "We ain't had no brownies in *months.*"

Kelly glanced at Anna, whose lips were pinched in an expression he was sorry to recognize—disapproval. That the kids had shared about the kitchen, or that Kelly was here? "That sounds like a pretty big problem," he said. "What else have you been missing out on?"

"Her lasagna—"

"And mac 'n cheese," Gina interrupted her brother.

"—and tacos and chili—"

"And mac 'n cheese!"

"—and pot roast," Mikey concluded glumly.

"Sounds pretty awful," Kelly said.

Growing up, his mama had thrived on having a hot supper on the table. He could only imagine how Anna felt being without her kitchen, because she wasn't offering up her feelings.

The living room was comfortable, lived in. A pair of couches faced each other, a low table in between. On one wall stood a television and next to it, a bookcase loaded with kids books of all shapes and sizes. That didn't surprise him. Anna had always loved to read.

Beyond the living room, a dining room was filled with a long table and six chairs. The lights were out, and although evening sunlight slipped through the blinds, he couldn't see into what must be the kitchen beyond.

"Can I see it? The kitchen?" he asked.

She hesitated.

"You asked me to find you some help," Paul said.

Her pinched expression made it clear she wasn't happy for the reminder.

"When Kelly told me he used to know you and what his vocation was, I figured we might have a solution for you."

"Hmm." Her lips flattened, turning white around the edges. It was clear she wasn't comfortable with Kelly here, in her home.

But if he could get into that kitchen, if he could explain... maybe she'd give him a chance to make things right.

He lifted the notepad of gridded paper. Had his trusty tape measure clipped to his belt. "I can draw up some sketches, see what we can do about your kitchen."

"Why don't you show him, Anna?" Paul said. "It's been

awhile since I've had time to talk to the kids. They can tell me all about their big plans for the summer."

Mikey and Gina latched on to the minister as he sat down on one of the couches.

Anna watched the kids for a moment, but he wondered if her mind weren't elsewhere. The memories were so thick in the room, it was a wonder the minister and the kids could hear each other over them. Which ones were flitting through Anna's mind right now? Because she certainly wasn't listening to the kids' jabbering, not with that look on her face.

After a deep breath—and if he could guess, a prayer—she lifted her gaze to his, nodded once, and turned. He followed her through the dining room into the kitchen.

She flipped on the light, and he couldn't help whistling at what he saw.

Someone had ripped out the countertops and most of the linoleum flooring, leaving the cabinetry open from the top. The electric stove had been disconnected and moved away from the wall. It now stood in the center of the room. The sink had also been removed and a gaping hole left in the cabinets beneath the sink, pipes exposed.

All of it had been done poorly. Old glue remained on the floor where it should have been scraped away. The cabinets had been banged up, damaged. One door hung off its hinges.

But it was all fixable. With enough time.

"So your contractor abandoned the job?" Paul had told him so, but he wanted to hear it from her.

"Yes."

"Did he leave behind any supplies? Have you purchased anything?"

"No." Could she sound any more reluctant to answer him? Probably not.

So the man, whoever he was, had done some demo and got out.

"What kind of work do you normally contract for?" She crossed her arms, remaining in the doorway as he stepped into the room and took out his tape.

"Commercial, mostly. But that doesn't mean I don't know my way around a kitchen."

He took measurements, and she fell quiet as he stretched the tape and scribbled in his notebook, sketching out a rough footprint of the kitchen. His mind was whirling —probably a defense mechanism—imagining what it might look like if he shifted the fridge a couple feet to the left and installed a dishwasher that was noticeably missing.

When he was done, he looked up to find her arms still crossed, a defensive posture if he'd ever seen one.

"I can't afford to pay a contractor's fee all over again."

She meant to scare him away. The tactic was so blatant that he leveled a gaze on her.

At least she had the grace to blush.

"Are you pursuing restitution from small claims court?"

Her chin came up again. "Yes, but I may not ever get my deposit back. That's why I asked Paul if he could find me someone who could at least get it back in working order—for cheap."

He turned a slow circle in the kitchen. "It's a great space. It'd be a shame to just make it livable." He spread his hands, gesturing to the long wall where the fridge and the cabinets remained. "I can see this as the main workspace. New backsplash, maybe a butcher-block counter. Or granite."

"I can't pay you."

She'd been just as proud and independent as a freshman in college. It was one of the first things he'd noticed about her, and it sparked unexpected joy in him to realize those characteristics were still there.

"I'll do the work for free, if you can afford the supplies."

Her eyes narrowed. "Why?"

Breath caught in his chest. This was it. The moment he'd been waiting five years for. Confession time.

ANNA SAW how his eyes cut to one side and waited for the inevitable excuse. Or outright lie.

This was Kelly, after all.

The man who'd charmed her, but quickly shown a side she'd had no interest in—his partier side.

But to her shock, he straightened his shoulders slightly and looked her right in the eye.

"I made a lot of mistakes. For years. I hurt you, and I'm sorry."

Her chest tightened up. For long moments, she felt as if she couldn't breathe.

"So... what? This is penance? You're going to fix my kitchen to earn my forgiveness?"

She hadn't meant the words to sound so cold, hadn't meant to snap at him like that, but his statement surprised her. Angered her, really. She didn't like feeling vulnerable. She didn't like *being* vulnerable, and if this kitchen proved nothing, it proved she was that.

And she didn't like the expectations he'd laid on her with both his presence and his apology.

"There's nothing I could do to deserve your forgiveness," he said quietly, and she had to look away from the shadows in his eyes. Her gaze fell to the side, and she saw the clench of his fist at his side.

"But I'd like to do something tangible. If it wouldn't be too much of a bother for me to be in your home. Working in your home."

She shook her head, thoughts whirling and a little panicked. "It's not necessary."

She couldn't think about him here, in the house where she and Ted had spent most of their married life. Where Gina had been born.

"At least let me draw up a sketch. You might change your mind when you see what the kitchen could be."

She'd already dreamed of what her renovated kitchen could be, and those plans had gone up in smoke like so much had since Ted's death.

Before she could give a final "no," thundering footsteps announced that the children had had enough of Paul's company.

Kelly seemed to understand how upset she was and made his way through the house and out the front door without saying goodbye. Numb, unable to focus, she trailed through the house and onto the porch. The kids ran around crazily in the yard as Paul lingered on the steps.

She couldn't imagine what Kelly had told him about their past. The minister certainly wasn't a pushover and was protective of his congregation. Last year when an online scammer had tried to steal money from one of their elderly members, he'd helped sort out the situation before any money had been lost.

"You've been looking for someone to help you repair the kitchen," Paul said.

She clung to her elbows, had her arms wrapped around her middle. "Yes, but..." *Not him.*

"Are you afraid of him? Any reason you should be?"

At that, she had to shake her head. "It was never... like that. He liked to party. Liked to drink. He was never mean or abusive, just someone I... didn't want to be around." That was partly it. She and Ted had fought about it frequently.

"He's clean."

She shook her head slightly before she'd even realized she'd done it.

Paul sighed, maybe at her unforgiving spirit. "He put me in contact with his sponsor, with the program he's worked."

Kelly had been in AA? Or something like it?

"He's one of the leaders in their program now. He's

not the same college kid you knew. Maybe God sent him to you."

Did God really care about her kitchen being repaired?

But she couldn't argue that Kelly's appearance held providential timing.

Her birthday was in three weeks, and the one thing she'd wanted more than anything else was a brand new kitchen and to host a party like the ones she and Ted had hosted together.

It looked like she might get her wish. But with Kelly? Why would God play that trick on her?

CHAPTER 2

"*H*e offered to fix your kitchen for *free?*"

Anna's gaze flew around the interior of the coffee shop, which was, thank heavens, sparsely populated at this time of midmorning. Most patrons at this hour came in, visited the counter, and left.

Mikey and Gina sat two tables away, heads bent over the table. Gina had a coloring book in front of her, and Mikey a video game. That should give her about ten minutes to chat with Melody and Lila. Lila had easily slipped into friendship with the two of them.

"I think he's looking to assuage a guilty conscience," Anna said, stirring the straw in her coffee cup. In the background, a fancy coffee machine hissed and spat.

"So..." Melody's leading comment trailed off, but it was Lila who continued.

"Why don't you let him?" She tossed her braid over her shoulder.

"It's... complicated."

The other two women sat side by side across from Anna, and now they exchanged a loaded glance.

"Complicated as in... he's attractive and you haven't really been interested in anyone since Ted?" Melody asked.

She *had* felt something last night when she'd first seen Kelly. It had been more of a punch than anything else.

He still had the looks he'd been graced with back in their college days, but looks weren't everything.

"Complicated as in Ted almost broke our engagement because of him." Not to mention the knock-down fight they'd had on their *wedding night* because of Kelly's actions.

"You've wanted your kitchen redone since before Ted passed," Melody reminded her. Three pairs of dangly earrings danced as her head bobbed in animation. "And sunk all that money into it."

With nothing to show for it. She'd gotten scammed. It still left a bitter taste in her mouth every time she thought about it.

"If it were me, I'd let someone work for free to finish the project," Lila said. Of course she'd say that. Impulsive Lila wouldn't have considered it for more than thirty seconds.

"Even if seeing that someone every day would bring back painful memories?" Anna sipped her coffee and let her eyes slide to the kids, who were, amazingly, still sitting in the booth.

Lila's eyes shadowed. Anna hadn't meant to touch a nerve. She still wasn't clear on Lila's reasons for coming back to town. After her enigmatic comment about being the prodigal, Lila hadn't visited her family's ranch since her arrival.

Melody had moved to Redbud Trails right around the time Anna and Ted had moved into town five years ago. Being one of very few women around her age, after Ted had died, they'd become as close as sisters.

But it was clear neither woman understood just what Kelly had been to her in the past.

Bells at the door jangled and out of habit, Anna swept a glance behind her.

And promptly sank down in the booth, shading her face with one hand. Heart thudding, she looked up to see her two friends' eyebrows raised, obviously trying not to smile.

"It's him," she mouthed.

"What was that?" Melody asked, maybe a shade too loud.

But anything Anna might have said was muted by Mikey and Gina's joyful shouts.

"Mr. Kelly!"

With any hope of him remaining oblivious to her presence evaporating, she sat up. Too slowly to nab either of her children as they raced past the booth toward the contractor.

She heard the tone of Kelly's greeting but couldn't make out his words.

"He's more than attractive," Melody whispered. "He's hot!"

Facing off with her friends and their dancing eyes

hurt her stomach, but turning to check on her babies even more so.

They stood on each side of Kelly, talking a mile a minute, beaming up at him.

KELLY HAD SEEN Anna's truck, the same one that had been parked outside her farmhouse last night, and turned in to the coffeehouse's small lot before he could talk himself out of it.

If he'd been smart, he would've headed out of town after her cool reception last night. He'd come to Redbud Trails to make amends for their shared past, and in the depths of his soul, he'd hoped for forgiveness.

He'd not only not been forgiven, but he was pretty sure if not for Paul, she'd have ordered him off her property. She hadn't agreed to let him help. And he had no reason to believe she would. Ever.

But apparently she could still render him stupid, because he'd stayed up until the wee hours of the morning furiously sketching the changes he'd like to make in her kitchen.

He held the sketch in his shaking hands, trapped between her children as they shot rapid-fire questions at him. His eyes adjusted to the dim interior after being out in the bright midmorning sunlight, bringing the modern decorations into focus.

"Have you ever built a tree house?" from Mikey.

"D'ya use a hammer? And a drill?" from the little girl, Gina.

He felt the weight of Anna's gaze from several feet away, where she sat with two women, who were grinning. He couldn't see Anna's face, so he decided to take her friends' grins as a good sign.

"I've never built a tree house, no. And I use a lot of tools."

Mikey strangely looked disappointed, but Gina lit up like a Christmas tree. "Cool!" She ran over to Anna. "Mr. Kelly has lots of tools, just like daddy used to!"

He waved off the barista behind the counter. He was so wound up that coffee would give him jitters.

He shored up his courage and followed Gina, getting a good look at Anna as Mikey tagged along just behind him. Her blonde hair hung between her shoulders and chin and had some curl at the ends. Her brown eyes shadowed as she considered him.

But her friends didn't seem to notice.

"Hi," the red-headed one said. "You must be the contractor Anna's been telling us about. Anna's friend from college."

Anna whirled back to face her friends. He couldn't see her face, but could guess at the expression she pulled.

She'd called him her friend?

Suddenly his heart was thudding in his ears like he was a teenager talking to his first crush.

"I'm Kelly."

"Lila."

"Melody."

Anna didn't look up at him. Maybe the redhead had assumed the *friend* part.

"You mind if I sit down for a minute?" he asked.

The brunette across the table smiled even more widely. "Why not?"

He thought Anna muttered, "I mind," but she inched over just enough for him to squeeze on the edge of the vinyl seat. His knee brushed against Anna's, and she scooted farther toward the wall. Gina clambered up into the empty booth behind them, standing so she could look between their shoulders to the table.

Kelly laid the three sheets of paper out on the slightly-sticky table surface, arranging them to show the 3D rendering of her kitchen as he'd imagined it.

"Oh, wow," Lila murmured, even though she was viewing it upside-down.

"Mom! It's a brand new kitchen. Lookit!" From his elbow, Mikey was bouncing up and down. Another pang of hope hit Kelly's heart, hard.

But Anna's head was down, and she remained silent.

He wanted to do this for her. More than he'd wanted anything in a long time. Maybe it was asking for heartache, because he knew if she allowed him to renovate her kitchen, it didn't mean she would forgive him.

But a remnant of the old Kelly, the one who had dared to dream big, wouldn't let him give up yet.

ANNA STARED AT THE SKETCH, aware of the expectant silence at the table.

They were all waiting on her to say she liked the sketch, the idea of her new kitchen.

And that was the problem.

She didn't like his idea. She loved it.

How had he intuitively known that she'd wanted something more modern? He'd sketched the upper cabinets lighter and the lower ones darker. A new backsplash made of small tiles, and new granite counters. Let her wipe up her drool now. And stainless steel appliances rounded out the space that looked nothing like her torn-apart kitchen now.

How had he known? They hadn't even talked through any details last night, only her nonexistent budget.

Gina shifted from the booth behind, jostling Anna's shoulder and breaking her fixation on the drawing.

She flicked a glance up to see Lila and Melody watching her. She didn't have the guts to glance in Kelly's direction, not with the hush that had fallen over the table.

"It's nice," she offered.

"Nice?" Lila echoed, disbelief clear in her tone.

"I can come up with something else—"

"It's exactly what you wanted," Melody burst out.

She wrinkled her nose at her friend.

"Yes," Lila said. "Of course, her answer is yes."

But she felt Kelly's gaze acutely. Waiting for her answer. "Annie?"

No one had called her that in years—except Ted.

"Mom, you should let Mr. Kelly fix our kitchen," Mikey said with the simplicity of a child.

Everyone thought she should agree.

And there was a part of her that wanted to.

But... Kelly.

Finally, she dared to look at him. She hadn't gotten this close to him last night. His caramel eyes were the same, with a few more lines creasing the corners. Maybe a few more shadows—ones that she didn't want to think about for too long. His lips dipped in a half-smile that told her he understood her reluctance more than anyone else at the table.

She didn't want to need him.

But she did.

"Fine," she agreed, looking back down at the drawing. Her heart thumped loudly in her ears. "When will you start?"

CHAPTER 3

*T*he sun was a bright ball just over the horizon as Kelly turned his pickup toward Anna's place the next morning.

He was really doing this.

Boy, there was nothing out here. Just cattle-dotted fields on both sides and the ribbon of dirt road kicking up dust in his rearview.

He burned his lips on the to-go coffee he'd picked up at the diner. The proprietor—apparently also the cook, because he'd come out from the kitchen in a grease-stained apron—had pestered him about renovating the diner's interior. He must've overheard the conversation from yesterday.

Kelly hadn't planned to stay in Redbud Trails after he'd made amends with Anna.

But he also hadn't planned on the spark of attraction that still flamed between them.

She'd barely looked at him that first night, but there had been no mistaking it as they'd sat next to each other in the diner. Awareness had skittered up his arm and across his spine when their elbows had brushed.

She'd avoided his gaze most of the time, but when their eyes had met, just for a moment...

He'd felt that connection clear to his toes.

He'd come to Redbud Trails to make amends. He'd known about Ted, had learned about the other man's death through a friend of a friend, but he'd thought whatever had been between him and Anna had died long ago.

He didn't have any business hoping that something might grow between them in the two or three weeks he was here.

She didn't seem to *want* to feel anything for him, if her manner were any indication.

Regardless of what she felt, he couldn't stop his attraction.

He'd had relationships after her. Just nothing that lasted. In the back of his mind, there'd always been Anna.

He had to stay grounded. He'd checked in with his sponsor via text first thing. There was a chance this could all go bad—like it had when he'd tried making amends with his old man.

Could he handle it if Anna turned her back on him? He prayed it wouldn't happen. She was lucky number thirteen—the last of those he'd wronged in a major way. Part of his recovery program was to accept responsibility for what he'd done and attempt to make amends with those he'd wronged.

Starting with rebuilding her kitchen. And hopefully her trust. And then asking her to listen.

His mind was so focused on his mission and half-stuck in the past that he almost didn't see the cows strung across the road until it was too late. He slammed on the brakes, and his truck fishtailed slightly, but came to a stop well away from the milling animals. Thank goodness.

There were a lot of them. All blocking the road to Anna's place. He gauged the short distance from where he was to where he knew the road turned left up ahead. These could be Anna's cows.

Where had they come from? He spotted a downed line of barbed-wire on the north side of the road just ahead.

They didn't seem to be in any hurry to move, and there was nowhere for him to go.

He rolled down his window and shouted. Banged his fist against the side panel of his door.

The nearest cows looked at him placidly, seeming content to lower their heads to the grass at the side of the road. Unmoving.

He groaned.

He'd managed to pry Anna's phone number from her before he'd left the diner yesterday, and now he dialed it on his cell phone, still leaning on his elbow out the truck window.

She didn't say hello. "You're backing out?"

He was so surprised he chuffed a bark of laughter—but her verbal shot struck low in his gut. "I'm stuck in traffic."

There was a beat where he couldn't help but wonder if this whole thing was a mistake.

But he'd promised to fix her kitchen, and he'd broken enough promises in his life.

He waited for her to say something. When all he got was silence, he continued. "There's a couple dozen cows spread out across the road. Any chance they belong to you?"

Another beat, and then she was shouting, "Mikey! Gina!" loud enough that he had to pull the phone away from his ear.

The line went dead. He looked at the phone as if it could tell him whether she'd hung up on him or the connection had been lost.

What now? No doubt he could come at the road to her place from the opposite direction—if he could get his phone's GPS to give him directions this far from civilization—but if these were her animals, wouldn't she need help getting them back where they belonged?

It wasn't ten minutes later when she came flying across the plain on horseback. Was that Gina behind her, clinging to Anna? Anna's hair flew out in a golden streamer behind her hat, and when she got closer, he could see the determination firming her mouth.

There was Mikey on a second horse, following fast behind her.

Kelly got out of his truck, intending to greet her or *something*, but she only waved him off.

Dismissed.

Irked, he watched her send Mikey carefully over the bowed fence. She dismounted on the road side, leaving Gina in the saddle, calling after Mikey to watch out for the temperamental bull.

Anna had leather gloves to protect her hands as she straightened a fallen post made out of weathered wood and tugged the fence back into place.

Meanwhile, Mikey rounded the cows and came up behind them on the far side, furthest from Kelly's truck, clucking and talking to them.

If they were moving them toward the red gate just up the pasture a bit, Kelly could help. He took off his ball cap and walked up to the nearest animal, holding both arms wide and waving the cap. "Hooey!" he called to it. "Move along."

Anna had re-mounted and was crossing behind him on her horse, and he distinctly heard a feminine giggle.

He glanced over his shoulder and, sure enough, her lips were twitching. Her cowgirl hat shielded her eyes, but he imagined them dancing. At his expense.

Gina, clinging to her mom's waist, wasn't hiding her giggles at all.

Anna cleared her throat. "What're you doing?"

"Helping. I guess I'm doing it wrong?"

She didn't confirm it, but her twitching lips were enough.

"Where'd you learn that, city boy?"

"TV, I guess." He let his arms fall to his sides and backed toward his truck as Anna and Mikey pushed the cows up the road.

"I'll meet you at the house," she said, and left him behind.

He stood next to his truck, feeling distinctly unnecessary. About a quarter mile up the road, Mikey jumped off his horse and opened the red gate, and Anna hustled the cows through.

He climbed into the truck and drove slowly toward them, not wanting to scare the horses.

With his window still down, he leaned out over his elbow. "You want me to fix the fence? I can run to town and get a post." And something to set it with. He hadn't fixed this type of fence before, but he'd wouldn't admit that to her.

"I'll handle it," she said over her shoulder.

And what he heard was, *I don't need you.*

His chest burned against the sting of her words, but he shrugged and put on an easy smile. If she wanted to keep him in the kitchen, that's where he'd stay.

He waited to make sure she'd gone through the gate and was back on her horse before he drove up the dirt road and turned into the long drive that would lead to her farmhouse.

Then he sat in his truck for long minutes, praying and breathing.

ANNA MET Kelly at the back porch. With the morning sun

at his back haloing his brown curls, she was hit with a bolt of attraction and a sense of déjà vu so strong she lost her breath. His T-shirt defined his shoulders and pecs, and his jeans were worn in all the right places.

She averted her eyes, focusing instead on his dusty work truck. The barn. The fields beyond. This was her world.

But as he neared, she could smell soap and man, and the ball of fire in her gut sharpened her tone. "What do you need from me?"

"How about a good morning?"

His unhurried, warm drawl brought her head up, but when she would've snapped at him, Mikey ran onto the porch, his boots thudding against the wood planks.

"Mr. Kelly!"

He plowed right into Kelly's gut, a full-force hug that had the man stepping back once for his balance.

Kelly's expression showed surprise before he looked down. His hand hovered above Mikey's head before he ruffled Mikey's hair. Almost as if he weren't sure of his welcome.

When he looked back up at Anna, his eyes *burned*.

And she swallowed back the harsh words she wanted to say at his genial greeting.

Kelly cleared his throat. "Where's your sister?"

"Inside eating breakfast."

Gina loved her food and had been frustrated when she'd been interrupted to gather up the cattle.

"Can I help you build?" Mikey's voice lilted, full of hope.

She waited for Kelly to brush him off, to tell Mikey the kitchen wasn't a place for a little boy, but he looked straight at Mikey. "I've got some projects that would be perfect for you, but not today. How about I let you know when I'm ready for you?"

"Tomorrow?"

"We'll see."

At least he hadn't promised. What if Kelly didn't even show up tomorrow?

She reached out and put a hand on Mikey's shoulder. "We'd better go in and finish eating too. Let me know if you need anything."

She said the words out of politeness, but she didn't meant them. Not really.

And Kelly knew it. She saw the realization in his eyes, the small tilt of his lips.

But he didn't tease or cajole or fuss like the old Kelly might've.

Which threw her off even more.

She ushered Mikey back into the liveable part of the house and tried to forget about the man working in the kitchen.

It proved impossible. He had hung plastic sheeting over the doorway—not that she'd walked through the dining room with the express purpose of spying—and the noises coming from inside resonated throughout the house.

She spent an hour in the barn, mucking out stalls and keeping an eye on Mikey and Gina, who frolicked in the pasture beyond.

She was using the hose from the spigot near the barn to spray clean some rubber buckets when Kelly stepped outside and stood at the edge of the back porch in plain view.

He slugged a bottle of water, and it was impossible to ignore the breadth of his shoulders, the definition of his chest beneath his T-shirt.

She squeezed the spray nozzle with more force than was perhaps necessary.

And then another vehicle drove up, a battered old Geo Metro she didn't recognize. In a small town like Redbud Trails, that was saying something.

A lanky young man got out of the truck and joined Kelly at the porch, then followed him inside.

She stifled her curiosity for another two hours, but when she'd settled the kids in their rooms for mandatory afternoon quiet time, she couldn't contain it any longer.

She dawdled her way into the dining room, pretending to be looking for... something.

Light and the rumble of male voices filtered through the plastic curtain, along with the scraping sound that she would probably hear in her sleep for nights to come.

When they didn't seem to hear her thundering heart or sense her presence after several minutes, she gave in and ducked through the plastic.

She stopped just inside the door. The young man— whom she definitely wasn't acquainted with—was wielding a long-handled scraper of some sort, and Kelly was on his knees—wearing some kind of pads—with a short-handled scraper in hand.

He looked up, his eyes open and warm and a smile stretching across his mouth. "You finally decided to stop loitering out there?"

"I..."—*didn't think you'd noticed me.* "I was just checking on you. Guys."

He sat back on his feet, allowing his tool to fall to the floor as his hands rested casually on his thighs. "We're doing good."

She jerked her chin toward the young man. "Who's this?"

The kid—he couldn't be older than eighteen or nineteen—pulled an earbud out of his ear and stuck a hand out to her. "I'm Tim."

She shook his hand out of habit more than anything else. "Anna."

Tattoos wrapped around his arm in a full sleeve, and there were piercings in both of his ears. His pants were too baggy, his hair too shaggy, and he didn't quite meet her eye.

Who was he? And why did Kelly have him working here? Tim wasn't the kind of guy she would willingly invite into her home, where she had impressionable kids.

"What are you guys doing?"

"Scraping," Tim said, and his voice was laced with disgust.

"Hey, it's gotta be done," Kelly said. "And you're getting paid."

Tim muttered something beneath his breath that sounded a lot like *not enough.*

But her attention had returned to Kelly, who was watching her with an enigmatic look on his face.

"The old linoleum was already gone," she said. She didn't understand why they were wasting time scraping the floor. It seemed unnecessary.

He didn't smile, but his eyes held hers. "Your old contractor left behind a lot of glue. We've got to clear it all away—get rid of all the old gunk—before we can lay new tile. Otherwise the new floor won't be right."

His words seemed to ring with meaning for more than just her kitchen, and she grew uncomfortable under the intensity of his gaze. She averted her eyes.

"Well. I'm glad you know what you're doing."

She ducked back through the plastic, but not before she heard his quiet, "I hope I do."

Heart beating loudly in her ears, she walked through the lower level of the house and stepped onto the front porch. She wrapped her arms around her middle, just trying to hold on.

Kelly seemed determined to do a good job on her kitchen. She should be happy for that, right?

But doing a good job might mean he would be around longer.

And she really didn't want that.

Kelly stirred up all those old feelings from their college days. She'd liked him, *really* liked him. And her feelings had been on the cusp of growing into something more when they'd had a disastrous first—and last—date.

Somehow, he could still melt her with a look. His smile sent tingles all the way down to her toes.

But she wasn't the same young woman any more, and she had Mikey and Gina to think about.

Plus, she couldn't forget that disastrous date. She couldn't trust Kelly to be in her life again, not as anything more than her contractor.

Could she?

CHAPTER 4

On Saturday morning, Anna had settled on the couch with a sad, reheated cup of coffee from the Coffee Hut—she'd bought a thermos when she'd been in town yesterday since no kitchen meant no coffeemaker—watching cartoons with the kids when the sound of an electric drill shocked her into spilling coffee onto her shirt.

"Mr. Kelly!" Mikey shot off the couch, cartoon forgotten. Gina was glued to the TV.

With a sigh, Anna called after her son, "Stay out of Kelly's way."

She was on her way to the stairs when Mikey yelled, "Mom!" and she detoured into the dining room, heart pounding.

The drill had gone silent. Had Mikey been hurt?

But he stood in the dining room, bouncing on the balls of his feet and his eyes alight. Kelly was behind him, in the doorway, holding the plastic sheeting away.

She became instantly conscious of the coffee stain that was spreading and the fact that the shirt it was spreading across was one of her rattiest ones. Ted had worn it when they'd first been married. She was still in her pajama bottoms. There were dirty dishes—the remnants of their breakfast—still strung across the dining table.

Because it was Saturday.

And he wasn't supposed to be here.

Kelly's lips twitched, but he didn't say anything as she crossed her arms over her chest.

"It's the weekend," she said inanely.

He nodded, expression serious. "So it is."

"Mr. Kelly said I can work with him today as long as you said it was okay, so is it okay, Mom?"

Her eyes cut between man and boy. Mikey's hopeful puppy-dog expression reminded her so much of Ted.

"Puleease?"

"I don't think we need to be in Kelly's way while he's working."

She knew just how much of a distraction Mikey could be and couldn't imagine Kelly wanting his *help*.

"It'll be fine," Kelly said easily.

"But what about...?" The other guy. *Tim*. She didn't know anything about the young man and wasn't sure she wanted Mikey around him. What if he were a bad influence?

She tried to glance past Kelly, but his broad shoulders filled the doorway, and the plastic sheeting behind his head make it impossible to see.

Kelly seemed to read her thoughts, as usual. "I gave Tim the day off, so I could really use the extra help."

Sure he could.

Mikey went on his tiptoes, eyes pleading, as if he could sense her wavering.

"I guess it couldn't hurt—"

"Yes!" Mikey pumped a fist in the air. "Thanks, mom. You're the best!" He rushed forward and threw his arms around her.

She met Kelly's eyes over Mikey's head, trying to warn him silently that if anything happened to her baby she would not be happy.

His eyes darkened, but he smiled when Mikey quickly turned back to him.

The plastic descended, and she felt a pang as if more than just a thin piece of see-through curtain separated them.

Mikey was growing up, and she couldn't help that, but this was more.

Did Mikey gravitate toward Kelly because he missed his dad? Needed a man in his life?

She'd been wrapped up in her own grief after Ted's death and then focused on raising the kids and surviving their day-to-day lives as a single mom.

Did Mikey have an unfulfilled need that she'd ignored?

It hurt to think it might be so. Panged when she heard the rumble of Kelly's voice—though she couldn't make out his words—and Mikey's answering chatter.

There were no answers to be found staring at the

plastic where man and boy had disappeared. She made herself go upstairs and change into her favorite pair of fitted jeans and a checked button-up shirt.

Even if she felt muddled about Kelly's presence and Mikey's pull toward him, she could look decent.

She wasn't dressing to draw Kelly's notice.

She wasn't.

"AND THIS IS THE ROPE LADDER..."

Kelly sat next to Mikey, their feet dangling off the back porch as the boy showed him a detailed sketch of his dream treehouse.

In the distance, a cow lowed. Other than that and some bugs chirping, there was silence. No traffic. It was peaceful, especially with the bright blue sky overhead.

The boy had obviously spent hours on the drawing, as evidenced by the details of each board and even leaves on the tree branches as Kelly bent his head to look.

"A rope ladder might be kind of wobbly if your sister wanted to climb up."

Mikey pulled a face, and Kelly was hard-pressed to keep a smile off his face.

"I want the tree house to be boys only. Just for me and my friends."

He might think girls had cooties now, but wait until he got older.

"Hmm." Kelly thought about it for a minute. "But sisters can be fun sometimes, right? Plus, you've got to be real careful on a rope ladder. What if you're in a hurry to get up into your tree house? A regular old board ladder would be much faster."

Mikey kept his head down, looking at the picture, his index finger tracing the ladder he'd drawn. "I guess."

"Mikey?" Anna's voice carried through the open door to the kitchen.

"Out here!" Kelly called back.

Mikey jumped up and ran to meet his mom. He disappeared into the kitchen, but Kelly could clearly hear him. "Lookit! Mr. Kelly let me unscrew all the handles from the drawers and all the cabinet doors." Though he couldn't see past a few feet inside, Kelly could easily imagine Mikey pointing to the careful rows of screws, kitchen hardware and cabinet doors Mikey had stacked along one wall inside. The boy liked to organize.

"Oh, wow. That must have been a lot of turns on the screwdriver."

"I used the drill."

He felt more than saw her moving toward him, and then she appeared in the doorway, looking adorable in jeans tucked into her cowgirl boots. Scowling.

"You let him use the drill?"

She was riled. And it shouldn't make him want to smile, but it did.

"He's almost nine. Plenty old enough."

He could almost see the steam releasing out her ears, saw the wheels of her mind working behind her eyes. "But what if—?"

"I was watching him the whole time. He was careful." More careful than Kelly would have been at that age.

Somebody needed to rough up the kid a little, teach him how to get good and dirty.

"But what about the cabinets? What if the drilled slipped?"

He shrugged. "Then I'd fix it when I sanded off the old lacquer."

She'd run out of arguments, but her frown remained.

Mikey and Gina tromped loudly through the kitchen, finally pushing mom gently out of the way. They both shoved each other, and then Mikey jumped off the porch.

Gina moved to follow, and Kelly found himself stretching out his arm to catch her even as Anna swooped behind and stopped her with a hand to her shoulder.

"Stairs, young lady."

"Aww, mom." But Gina quickly obeyed and joined her brother in the grass. She took off to the barn, but Mikey turned back.

"Mr. Kelly, wanna come see my horse?"

He shouldn't. He knew Anna wanted him to stay in the kitchen and finish the job, but he'd been working hard for two and a half days, and a few minutes in the barn wouldn't hurt anything.

He found himself on his feet and trailing the boy toward the large red structure across the grassy yard.

Anna muttered as she took up the rear.

A short-furred dog ambled out to meet them as they neared the barn.

"That's Otis," Mikey said. "He's been mom's dog since before I was born."

The dog's tongue lolled out in a doggie smile as Kelly dropped a pat on its head and followed Mikey into the barn.

The interior was cool and shadowed, sunlight filtering in through the double doors thrown wide. The scents of hay and horses had his nose twitching, but he managed to ward off a sneeze.

Mikey gestured him closer to a stall door.

"This is Samson."

A huge brown head came over the stall door, and the horse lipped Mikey's shoulder.

"Wow. He's big."

Bigger than Kelly had expected. He'd seen Mikey riding that first morning when the cows had blocked him, but he hadn't realized how big the horse was compared to Mikey.

The horse snuffled Mikey's hair, and the boy laughed, ducking away from the animal. It swung its head toward Kelly, making a sort of *whuffle* sound.

He couldn't help it, he stepped back.

Mikey looked at him with wide eyes. "You scared of him?"

He hated to admit to the sweat trickling down the back of his T-shirt, but it seemed too late to hide his reaction.

"Kelly was a city boy back when I knew him before. You've still never ridden?"

He glanced over his shoulder to where Anna was fiddling with a latch on a stall across the barn aisle. Gina sat in an empty stall nearby, playing with a doll and singing to herself.

"No. I've never ridden."

"He won't hurt ya," Mikey said, and darn if he wasn't wearing that hopeful look he'd given his mother just this morning.

Kelly wanted to tell him *thanks, but no thanks*, but the boy had been earnest and funny all morning. And made Kelly feel stirrings he hadn't felt in a long time.

So he found himself stepping forward under Mikey's guidance and rubbing along the horse's smooth nose, just under the tuft of hair falling over its forehead.

The animal made another of those *whuffle* noises, but this time Kelly didn't step back. Even though he wanted to.

"He likes you." Mikey seemed happy about it, which made one of them.

Kelly glanced back to see Anna still struggling with the latch. She grunted and finally it popped free.

"I could look at that for you," he said.

She shook her head, not really answering.

"I got a great idea!" Mikey exclaimed.

He was almost afraid to ask.

"I could teach you to ride. Every cowboy needs to know how to ride."

He opened his mouth to explain that he wasn't a cowboy, but Mikey had moved further into the barn. "C'mon, the tack room is down here."

"I don't think—" How was a boy going to teach a grown man to ride?

"Mom can help. Won't you, mom?" Mikey turned his charm to his mother again, but when Kelly looked, Anna's gaze was on him.

And she looked to be stifling a smile, her lips pinched together.

His stomach flip-flopped just seeing the mirth in her eyes—even if it was directed at him.

He shook his head in silent beseechment, opening his palms toward her to show he didn't know how to deny her son.

"I'll help." She stood with her hands casually on her hips. Her eyes hadn't left him this whole time. "If you promise to really get on the horse."

Then the horse nudged him in the back with its nose, propelling him forward a step.

It seemed everyone thought he should do it.

ANNA HADN'T THOUGHT this through.

She'd seen Kelly standing there with a *help me* look on his face, frazzled, and she'd been so glad to have their roles reversed that she'd spoken up—agreed to Mikey's plan—without really thinking about it.

Hadn't thought about having to dust off Ted's old saddle, because Kelly's bum wouldn't fit on Mikey's child-sized one.

Hadn't thought about standing close, heads bent together as she showed him the reins.

Hadn't thought about their fingers tangling or the

zing that traveled up her spine and down every nerve ending.

She clearly hadn't thought about being eye-level with his muscled thighs or adjusting the stirrups for each of his feet. Touching him again, even if this time it was through layers of denim and leather boots. It was too intimate.

She blamed her son and the charm he'd inherited from his father.

While Gina played with her doll in the shadow of the barn, Mikey rattled off instructions on how to tell the horse what you wanted it to do, how to turn it, and even more, so much information that Kelly wouldn't possibly be able to remember.

When she stepped back, Kelly shifted in the saddle. Probably out of nerves, but it sent the horse forward a step, and, unprepared for the movement, Kelly weaved in the saddle.

"Whoa, boy," Mikey said, stepping in and taking hold of the bridle. Samson stilled, though his skin quivered.

She should have had Mikey take him out for a ride first to get some of his pent-up energy out. Although he was gentle, the horse liked to move, and he'd been cooped up in the stall since morning.

Kelly looked a little green.

"You okay, cowboy?" she asked. If he fell, he could be hurt, and what would that mean for finishing her kitchen?

"Fine," he said tightly.

But he wasn't the usual easygoing Kelly.

"You ain't afraid of heights, are you?" Mikey asked, intuitive as ever.

"Only a little," Kelly admitted.

And now she did have to stifle a laugh. She pressed the back of her hand against her mouth, but the motion didn't hide anything from Kelly, whose eye's flicked to her, then narrowed.

"You'll be fine, cowboy. You're only five feet off the ground."

She patted his leg and turned to go back to the barn. She had intended to take one of the other two mounts out for an afternoon ride before she'd gotten distracted by Mikey's idea.

She took Gina along with her as she circled the big field, keeping one eye on Kelly as he rode in stops and starts, Mikey trailing on the ground.

She couldn't hear him from this distance, but no doubt her son was chattering away.

She left them to it, confident that Samson would behave himself and that Mikey was horseman enough to keep Kelly from falling off.

She wrapped one arm around Gina sitting in front of her and let the mare have its head. Wind whipped through her hair, and Gina laughed with joy as the horse galloped over the property. Anna laughed with her.

They took their time, the movement and freedom a release that Anna definitely needed after having Kelly around the past few days.

But her mind kept circling to his nervousness around the horse, those moments of uncertainty. That he hadn't

49

blustered his way through it, pretending confidence, surprised her. The old Kelly would've.

Ted had been a city boy, too. After college and their wedding, they'd come back to Redbud Trails, were she'd grown up. Her dad had passed the year before Mikey was born and had left them the farm. Because there weren't that many jobs in Redbud Trails, they'd been thinking of looking for work in Oklahoma City, about two hours away.

But when Dad had passed, it had made sense to stay.

Plus, she'd loved it here from her earliest memories.

They didn't have enough land for a huge herd, and the cattle didn't make that much money, but she was able to supplement most years with a large garden that provided fresh vegetables, and she did some marketing freelance work on the side.

They'd done okay, but Ted had chafed under the pressures of running the farm. Not knowing if the weather would hold to provide a good crop through the growing season. Late nights during calving season when they might have to pull a calf.

She loved the lifestyle, loved the outdoors, but Ted had never really acclimated.

She hadn't seriously thought about remarriage since Ted's death two and a half years ago, but if she *was* thinking about it, she knew she didn't want another city boy for a husband.

It might take all her effort to run this place and take care of the kids, and sure she didn't have time for every job—like the fence that was falling down along the south side of the property—but she loved it.

If she *were* looking, she'd be looking for someone to partner with here, on the farm.

Good thing she wasn't looking.

ANNA RETURNED to the yard at a slower pace. Gina, having been lulled by the ride, had fallen asleep against her. Her arm had started to ache, holding the little girl steady, but she knew she wouldn't have many more moments like this. Both kids were growing up too fast— Mikey was already outgrowing the nicer jeans she'd bought him to wear to church on Sundays—and soon Gina would be riding on her own.

She was surprised to see Mikey on Pepper, the older gray mare that had been in her stall when Anna had taken off on her ride. He and Kelly ambled along, their mounts dallying across the field.

She could see Mikey's mouth moving, still chattering, though she imagined Kelly would be tired of it by now. She was surprised he hadn't taken off. What about his normal Saturday plans? Surely they hadn't included hanging out with a bright eight-year-old.

She reined in near the pair, noticing that Kelly's nose was a little pink from being in the sun. And his seat was more relaxed now. He looked more natural in the saddle, his thighs flexing. She averted her eyes, but her thoughts weren't as quick to follow.

She was just in time to hear Mikey expounding on the merits of a sturdy oak at the edge of the woods.

Still talking about his treehouse.

A lump rose to her throat. It was the last conversation he'd had with Ted before her husband had died unexpectedly of a brain aneurism.

She'd thought he'd forgotten about it until recently, when he'd learned Kelly was a builder. And now he seemed fixated on it.

If she had money to burn, she'd hire someone to build him a treehouse.

"I think you're right about that being the one," Kelly agreed. "The trunk is nice and wide and would support a structure like the one you want."

Mikey pushed his cowboy hat back on his head. "Do you think you could help me build it?"

"Mikey," she warned.

He knew better than to ask for something as huge as that.

But Kelly waved off her warning. "I'll build you one."

She gasped, his words like a punch to her solar plexus.

"Promise?" Mikey's jaw had firmed, and his tone spoke of his intensity in the request.

"I promise."

She wheeled her mount and headed back to the barn. She left her horse tied off for a few moments while she took the still-sleeping Gina inside and laid her on the couch. Then she returned to the barn to remove her horse's saddle and brush it down.

When Mikey and Kelly came in minutes later on foot and guiding their horses by the reins, she took the reins and sent Mikey inside to wash up.

She was too worked up to say a kind goodbye to Kelly, but, apparently, it was too much to ask for him to get in his truck and go home, because he came up beside her as she hauled Samson's saddle off.

The heavy weight strained the muscles of her arms as she turned to lug it to the small closet they used to store the tack.

Kelly was in her way.

"I can help," he said.

She brushed past him. "You've helped enough."

"What's that supposed to mean?" he called after her.

She ducked into the tack room and deposited the saddle on its pommel, stopping to take a moment and breathe through the ache in her chest.

She didn't want to say something she'd regret, but when she returned to the barn proper, words spewed out before she could temper them.

"You shouldn't have promised Mikey you'd build a treehouse," she snapped.

He looked so earnestly confused that for a moment, a completely different pain took her heart.

"You don't want me to build him a treehouse," he repeated slowly. "But you're letting me reno your kitchen...?"

His words trailed off in a question.

"If you stick around to finish it."

Her barb struck true. She saw the light dim in his eyes. "You still think I'm going to flake out," he said flatly.

She shrugged and crossed her arms across her middle, looking past him. She still needed to brush both horses and put them away with grain and water, but she couldn't do that with him here.

"I can't make you believe me, but I will finish this job," he said. The warmth had gone out of his voice, replaced by something else she couldn't identify. "And that tree house is important to him."

"I know it is!" Without meaning to, she was almost shouting the words at him, and she was surprised to find her vision blurred by tears.

Of course the treehouse was important to Mikey. It was a link to his dad. But she didn't want *Kelly* to be the one to give it to him.

KELLY SLAMMED INTO HIS TRUCK, shaking and unable to catch his breath.

He'd followed Anna into the barn, hoping that with the way she'd opened up today—she'd even smiled at him once!—she would be receptive to hearing him out and maybe start working on the forgiveness he craved.

Instead she was angry and tearful about the promise he'd made to Mikey. He didn't understand where her emotions were coming from, but he was smart enough to realize he'd stepped in something.

He should've found a different way to make amends.

Should have just sat her down and said what he needed to say.

And not tried to prove anything to her.

That was his big mistake here, wanting her to see, to believe he'd changed. That and letting his heart engage.

He liked Mikey. He hadn't interacted much with Gina, who seemed content to play in her own little world, but Mikey had welcomed him. Made him feel wanted. Kid had even invited Kelly to the church picnic tomorrow.

And if that didn't open up old wounds...

He drove back to the tiny motel in Redbud Trails, mulling it over in his head.

His was still the only vehicle in the parking lot. Probably the only room rented.

He showered away the day's grime and thought about walking down Main Street to the diner, but he wasn't hungry.

He let his hands run down his face.

He wasn't hungry, he was hung up on Anna.

Again.

And she—still—didn't want him around.

CHAPTER 5

*T*he little church in Redbud Trails had a potluck dinner about every quarter, and this go around it just happened to be a picnic in the small community park where there was plenty of room for the kids to run and play. The ladies of the church—including Anna—had laid out the food under the pavilion's shade, and folks had spread their picnic blankets and lawn chairs across the grassy field. The rain the weatherman threatened seemed to be hanging back, though gray clouds dotted the sky.

Anna had seen Kelly in the worship service that morning, but he'd stayed to the back and kept his distance.

And it helped that Mikey had been too busy chattering with his best buddy Drew about the grand treehouse he was getting to notice Kelly's presence.

Which is why she was surprised to see Mikey towing him by the hand toward the picnic table she and Lila and Melody had appropriated. Gina had begged off to sit with a friend on a picnic blanket nearby. Melody and Lila went suspiciously silent, even as Kelly pulled back several feet away from the picnic table.

Then Paul appeared, clapping a hand on Kelly's shoulder. "Saw this young man trying to sneak out of the church building and twisted his arm to join in our potluck today."

Judging by Kelly's hesitation, arm-twisting was right.

"C'mon, I'm hungry, aren't you?" Mikey said, and she realized Kelly held a heaping paper plate and had a red plastic cup hanging precariously from his finger and a bottle of water tucked beneath his arm.

"Sure, why don't you sit with us?" Melody offered.

Anna swallowed the denial that rose to her lips.

One side of Kelly's mouth lifted in a rueful smile. "I'll find somewhere else."

"No!" Mikey whined, showing a rare unpleasant side.

"Mikey," she warned.

"Aw, c'mon Mom, please? Mr. Kelly's been so nice, and I want to talk to him about some modifications for my treehouse."

Heads turned, including Lila and Melody's. Probably wondering why she wasn't welcoming the handsome contractor with open arms.

Her face flushed with heat. Just what she needed—her son causing a scene.

"It's fine," she said quickly.

She was shocked when Kelly set his plate and the

bottle of water on the table and then squatted down face-to-face with Mikey.

"It's not respectful to whine at your mom if she tells you something you don't want to hear. I think that's a cowboy rule or something."

Mikey shot a look at her. "Sorry, mom," he mumbled.

If her face had been warm before, it was on fire now, watching Kelly having a *talk* with her son. Like his father might've, if Ted had still been alive.

It was on the tip of her tongue to tell him it wasn't his place, but he *had* been telling her son to respect her. That wasn't a message she wanted mixed in Mikey's mind.

Kelly's eyes cut to hers and then away as he maneuvered his long legs onto the concrete picnic bench and sat.

Mikey pulled a folded piece of notebook paper out of his pants pocket, but before he could spread it on the concrete surface, she interrupted. "Mikey, you need to eat."

Mikey stuffed a fresh strawberry from his plate into his mouth, tapping the paper with his other hand. "Thith va labber."

"Mikey," she admonished.

"Sowwy," her son said, finally chewing and then swallowing.

Kelly's eyes met hers, and they shared a smile. The pit of her stomach flip-flopped, and she focused her attention back on her plate.

She let Mikey carry the conversation for a few moments, but finally Mikey's appetite kicked in, and he attacked the hot dog on his plate. Without Mikey's voice filling the space, the silence seemed to spread.

A tall shadow fell over the table, and Anna looked up to see Ben Taylor, the foreman that ran the Andrews ranch, approach Lila. He was dressed in a cowboy's Sunday best, a button-up shirt over Wranglers with a white dress hat and a shine on his boots. He bent to talk to her.

With Lila on the opposite end of the table and caddy-corner, Anna couldn't make out his words, but Lila's face filled with color and her eyes sparked as she hissed something back to the cowboy.

The cowboy stuffed his hat on his head and strode away, tension in each line of his tall form.

Anna knew her brows were raised as Lila turned back to the table, her color still high. But Lila didn't offer up an explanation, just turned to Kelly with a wide, false smile. "Anna says you're doing a good job on the remodel."

His eyes cut to Anna's and then away. "She does, huh?"

KELLY DIDN'T THINK Anna had said any such thing. Not after the way they'd left things yesterday, with him stepping in a minefield he hadn't even been aware of and her in tears.

"Nothing much to see yet," he said. "The interesting parts come later, putting it all together."

Her friends at least wore open and friendly gazes, even if Anna's was conflicted.

"Are you going to do granite for the countertops?" the auburn-haired one—Melody—asked.

"Yep."

Anna's interest was piqued. He could tell by the way her head lifted slightly, even though she didn't look directly at him. "I can't afford that," she said to her plate.

"I can."

She looked up at him this time, and he could see the protest on her lips, but someone called out to her, and a woman surrounded by three identical young boys stopped to talk. Anna turned sideways to speak to her.

The sun slanting down highlighted the gold in Anna's hair, and she tucked some loose strands behind her ear.

For a moment, he got lost in the past.

During that first magical semester, they enjoyed an Indian summer and October came with long stretches of warm days. He'd wheedled until Anna agreed to a picnic in the quad. The sturdy oaks above their blanket were a canopy of orange and yellow leaves. Backpacks forgotten on the grass nearby, Anna was the only thing he could see.

He was hungover. That was nothing new.

The bright autumn sunlight only made his piercing headache worse. His shades helped, and an added benefit was the fact that they hid his bloodshot eyes.

But none of that mattered, because he was with Anna. Six weeks in to the semester, and he knew. He wanted to be with her for the rest of his life.

"What'd you get on Professor Dee's test?" she asked.

"C. You get an A?" It wasn't really a guess—she'd

gotten A's on every quiz. He knew because they sat together. The first time he'd sat on the front row. Ever. Even in elementary school he'd been a back-row kid.

And while Anna stayed wrapped up in the lectures, he stayed wrapped up in her.

"You should think about coming to study group." She bumped his shoulder, a friendly tap. "It's every Wednesday night."

He shrugged, smiling goofily down on her. "It's not my scene."

He could pull a C or maybe even a B just by coasting —and that was good enough for him. College was for fun and partying—and when he got around to it, studying. As little as he could get away with.

She dug into the small ice chest he'd bummed off a friend two apartments over. He'd spent twenty minutes this morning scouring it to get rid of the stench of alcohol.

"I can't believe you planned this." She was effervescent as she pulled out the two sandwiches and bags of potato chips he'd purchased at the caf before their ten a.m. class.

He couldn't believe it either. His usual m.o. with girls was hooking up at a party.

He couldn't even say he'd had a real first date.

But with Anna... he wanted it all.

She leaned forward, and her hair fell across his shoulder, sending sparks every which way.

"So..." he started.

She tilted her chin up, and they were only inches

away. If he leaned in—and if she didn't turn away—he could kiss her.

He wanted to kiss her.

But unlike all those one-night hookups that he could barely remember, something held him back.

"Do you want to go out with me Friday night?"

"Mr. Kelly!" Mikey's voice rang out and brought him back to the present. Thinking about Anna and what they'd shared probably wasn't the best idea. He still had to figure out how to get through the next few weeks of completing her kitchen when she didn't really want him there. And finish his apology.

The summer sun beat down on his head, and in jeans and a T-shirt, he wished for a pair of basketball shorts. He settled for taking a long swig from the plastic cup he'd filled with lemonade from a cooler beneath the pavilion.

Anna's eyes slid to him and away. And suddenly he couldn't take her suspicion and passive-aggressive treatment any longer. "What?" he demanded softly.

She shook her head, but her lips were pinched.

"Tell me."

She glanced toward her friends. He was aware of them listening in, but he didn't care.

"Your cup. It makes me think of..."

Of course. His drinking days and the fateful date. How many times had he filled countless cups like this from a keg?

Without a word, he took the cup and upended it in the grass behind the picnic table.

Her friends shared a glance. "What's that about?" Lila asked.

"I'm an alcoholic." He'd said it so many times, first in the recovery program and then as he'd worked to make amends with the twelve people on top of his list. "I've been clean for four years, six months and eleven days."

He looked straight at Anna. "But Anna doesn't trust that yet. So I don't mind proving it to her."

"Well you can't eat without a drink," Melody said. "You'll get dehydrated."

"Especially if you're eating Maude's jalapeño poppers," Lila said.

Not in the time it took him to finish his lunch, but it was nice that they cared. He tapped the half-full bottle of water he'd brought out of his truck earlier.

But Anna's eyes stuck on it as well. "Couldn't it be filled with something?"

Her words were tentative, almost as if she were afraid to speak them or maybe she didn't want to seem combative.

But she was talking to him. And she seemed more open than she had even yesterday before he'd messed everything up.

"Vodka," he said. It was clear and for the most part, didn't have a scent. "But it's not."

But he unscrewed the top and dumped the water where he'd just dumped the lemonade.

"Umm..." Melody said.

"It's 90 degrees out," Lila said.

"And you got jalapeños," Mikey said helpfully.

But his eyes were on Anna. He shrugged. "I'll live." It would be worth it if this stunt would get her one step closer to trusting him.

He munched on one of the breaded jalapeño bites. They weren't *that* spicy.

Until he swallowed.

And then fire burst on the back of his tongue and down his throat. Even his esophagus felt singed.

Mikey looked up at him, concerned. "Are you okay?"

The skin of his face started to burn even as his eyes watered.

"Yeughp." His affirmation sounded more like a croak than a word, so he tried clearing his throat. "Yes," he whispered. There. See, he could still talk.

Anna's friends' faces had creased with concern. He had no idea what Anna's face looked like—he wouldn't look at her, not now, acting like the idiot he was.

Maybe if he ate something else, it would help douse the fire. He had a small roll on his plate. Blindly, he reached for it and popped it in his burning mouth.

Too late, he realized it was another popper. It would be rude to spit it out, so he barely crunched into it and then swallowed.

Started coughing.

"Kelly."

That was Anna's voice, but he couldn't see her through the tears in his eyes.

Something cool and wet was pressed into his hand, and he didn't even think. He just drank, gulping the water.

When the water bottle Anna had thrust at him was empty and Mikey had run off for another one and returned, Kelly took the second bottle and upended it over his head, cooling his burning face and neck.

Finally blinking to clear his vision, with the fire in his mouth reduced to coals, he looked across the table.

Melody and Lila wore matching expressions of concern. Mikey, at his elbow, wore the same.

But it was Anna that he couldn't look away from.

She was smiling.

LATER, when the table had been cleared and Melody and Lila had gone, Anna lingered with Kelly at the picnic table. Mikey ran around with his friends in an impromptu soccer game, and Gina had gone home with her friend for a nap.

Clouds passed over the sun, dappling them with shade.

Anna leaned an elbow on the table. Kelly had shifted to stretch one long leg along the picnic bench, while the other tapped the ground. She remembered him always full of energy, always drumming fingers on the top of the desk or bouncing his knee beneath.

Even though his energy was the same, if she looked closer, the manic light in his eyes wasn't there anymore. He seemed more at peace with himself.

It made him even more dangerous.

"My home church in Oklahoma City is bigger," he was saying, his eyes following the soccer game. "The singles group usually has their own events, but I don't go all that often."

"Why not?"

His eyes shifted to hers. "It's... it can be... let's just say there are lots of women in the singles group looking to change their status."

Ah. He was trying to be polite and not come out and say that it was a meat market.

She shifted on the bench, pretending the stone was making her uncomfortable, but it was more the rock in her gut that provided discomfort. She was trying—and failing—not to imagine Kelly in the dating pool.

Which was ridiculous, because she had no claim on him and no business even thinking that she might.

He didn't seem to register her discomfort as he gazed at the families mingling. "This is... it's nice."

"Some families come and go," she said, with a silent but stern reminder to herself about *city boys*. "It's harder to make a living in a small town. Some families don't like the differences from the city." Or some men.

"Hmm."

He'd tilted his head to one side, considering her words. She remembered that about him, how he'd always listened to her with his full attention.

"What?" she asked.

He shrugged slightly. "Seems like there'd be room for a contractor or a builder in town. I've had several folks asking me if I was planning to stay, looking for work to be done on their homes or businesses."

Her stomach swooped low at the thought of Kelly staying. Making his life here.

But he very clearly hadn't said he was staying.

Now she was the one who focused on Mikey playing soccer. "You'd probably go crazy after a month here. There isn't much to do, no nightlife."

And the old Kelly she remembered had been all about the action.

"That's not really my scene anymore."

His slow words—and the memory of another time he'd spoken about *his scene*—drew her gaze reluctantly back to him.

Caught in the intensity of those toffee eyes, she couldn't make her voice work, so she nodded instead.

"Back then, I was looking for what I needed in all the wrong places," he went on. His eyes had gone shadowed. "But you might be surprised at the things I'm looking for now."

His words were too close to that *talk* he'd wanted to have the first night he'd appeared back in her life. She wasn't ready yet.

She cleared her throat. "So... what about your friend Tim? How do you know each other?"

At first glance, Kelly and Tim were different. Kelly was mostly clean cut, except for the long hair that teased at his collar. And Tim was... Tim. With his tattoos and piercings and the attitude she'd caught from his muttered words.

"I met Tim about eighteen months ago at—well, I guess that's his story to tell. He's worked with me off and on. He's got some things still going on in his life that... again, that's his business. But I figure the guy deserves a second chance. Everyone does, right?"

She wished she could agree, but she wasn't so sure.

After Kelly's easy admission today about the problems he'd had in the past, the way he'd said he wouldn't drink *anything* to prove to her he wasn't drinking alcohol...

It had muddled her thinking. She'd put Kelly into a box labeled *bad news* and these new revelations kept popping the lid open.

She'd wanted to keep him solidly in the past.

But he refused to stay there.

Did he want a second chance at friendship? At something more?

It was frightening to think about.

He'd already opened her eyes that Mikey might need more in his life than she could give alone.

Did she want her eyes opened that there might be something missing in *her* life too?

CHAPTER 6

"*C*ome on, come on."

Three days after the church picnic, Anna cranked the engine in her extended cab Ford pickup.

But it only clicked. *Click, click, click.*

Nothing.

"Mo-om, I'm gonna be late for practice!" Mikey's chin was on the back of her seat, his baseball cap skewed to one side. Gina kicked the seat behind her, right at Anna's lower back, but at least she wasn't complaining.

The humid air inside the cab of the truck was a sweltering oven. Afternoon sunlight slanted through the windshield and baked Anna's tension up a level higher.

"Mo-om!"

"Honey, I'm doing everything I can."

She popped the hood and got out. Moved around the front of the truck to stare at the engine. What was she doing? She didn't know anything about the mechanics of an engine.

It was too late to call Lila or Melody. By the time one of them came out to get them and then drove back to town, Mikey would have missed his practice.

"Problem?"

She whirled at Kelly's voice, heart pounding at the unexpected presence. She'd thought he was finishing up in the kitchen, around the far side of the house.

"Mr. Kelly!" Mikey must have crawled over the front seat, because he was leaning halfway out the driver's side window. "Our truck won't start."

"Uh oh. Want me to give it a listen?"

She sighed but figured he wasn't going away, so she brushed past him and got back in the truck. She didn't bother closing the door. Mikey scooted into the passenger seat. She turned the keys again, and again it just *click, click, clicked.*

From where he'd been bent over the engine, Kelly leaned around and waved for her to stop.

"Sounds like the battery," Kelly said.

"But, Mom, my practice..."

"You need to get to town?"

Anna stifled a second sigh as she looked between Mikey, who was so disappointed about missing his practice, and Kelly, who watched her with an expectant look on his face.

"Yes, we need to get to town."

He nodded.

Waited.

She said nothing.

"It's okay to ask for help." The words emerged

straight-faced, but when her chin jerked up, it was clear to see the spark in his eyes.

"It's taken me awhile to learn..." he continued. And raised his eyebrows, a clear challenge.

She stifled the growl that wanted to emerge.

Mikey's quiet, "Mo-om..." made her back teeth clench. Fine.

"Would you please drive me and the kids into town?" She might have gritted the words out from between her teeth, but she'd gotten them out.

But if he said one mocking thing...

"Glad to," was his quiet, pleased response. "I'll fire up the truck."

Mikey was already jumping out of the cab.

"Honey, grab your mitt."

"Oh, yeah!"

Mikey scrambled back up into the truck, and she reached inside for her purse and helped Gina out.

Rounding the house, she saw that Kelly had quickly sealed up the silver toolbox attached to the truckbed and closed the tailgate as the kids sprinted up to him.

"The inside is a bit of a mess. You'll have to pretend it isn't there."

Reluctantly curious, she opened the passenger door. The kids scrambled over the seat and rushed to buckle up in the back. The interior of his truck was probably cleaner than hers but boasted several fast food wrappers and a T-shirt crumpled next to the center console, where a notepad and what looked like outgoing bills made a messy pile.

It seemed like he was living out of his truck. And it was a reminder that he was only in town to work on her kitchen. He wasn't staying.

Kelly seemed to sense her hesitation. Their eyes met over the center console as she climbed in the passenger seat. Things had changed between them at the picnic on Sunday afternoon.

And she didn't know if she was ready for that.

THEY ARRIVED at the baseball park that had apparently been built by a rancher on his property. Nothing like the huge parks Kelly was used to in Oklahoma City, where multiple games and practices would go on at once.

Anna stood in the V of the open truck door and the cab, watching Mikey as he ran off to join his teammates.

She moved away momentarily to talk to another mom, gesticulating. With her back to him, he couldn't tell what she was saying. Didn't stop him from admiring the way her worn-out jeans hugged her curves.

She got back in the truck, the tense set of her shoulders betraying her.

"Mom, I want ice cream!" Gina said from the backseat.

"Maybe later, honey."

Maybe if he weren't here...?

She flicked a glance at Kelly. "I know it's a lot to ask, but would you be able to run me to the auto parts store? The nearest one is in Weatherford."

Stuck in the truck with Anna for another hour and a half?

"What about Mikey?"

"His friend's mom agreed to have him over. We can pick him up on our way home."

"In that case, I don't mind."

It was an understatement.

Those hours they'd spent talking Sunday afternoon had opened a door between them.

She'd stopped avoiding him. Oh, she didn't seek him out, but when she'd passed him on the way to the barn on Monday, she'd actually stopped and talked to him. Tim had been there, and she'd been friendly with the both of them.

She'd brought out some sweet tea late yesterday afternoon, claiming she had extra.

He'd been grateful for the chance to talk to her, even if it was about how the kitchen was progressing and whether they had a chance of getting any rain tonight.

And now this. He'd been teasing her earlier about asking for help, but he sensed that the independence he'd recognized from their college days had reared its head after Ted's death. He'd run into Melody at the coffee shop, and after he'd pried, she'd shared a little about how Anna had closed off, distanced herself for months until the grief had waned a bit.

He turned the truck toward the bigger town—still nothing like Oklahoma City or the even bigger Dallas, the familiar feel of tires on freeway soothing to him. The AC hummed, keeping them icy cool.

"You gonna fix the truck, Mommy?" Gina piped from the backseat.

"Umm..." She slid a glance to him. "I might have to break down and call Lucy." She turned to him. "She's the local mechanic."

A woman mechanic? Interesting. He kept his gaze on the highway. "Battery isn't hard to fix. Disconnect the old one and connect the new one. If it's something more than that, it's outta my league."

"Okay. Thank you." The soft expression of gratitude hit him straight in the solar plexus.

"Just helping a friend."

A mile passed in silence. A glance in the rearview showed Gina whispering to thin air.

His brows must've crunched together, because Anna looked over her shoulder and then sighed softly.

"She has an I-M-A-G-I-N-A-R-Y friend."

His lips twitched. "I see."

"Did you ever have one?"

He was a little surprised by the question but shook his head. "I don't think so. Did you?"

"My mom says I did, but I don't remember it. She says his name was Eric."

"I can imagine that about you."

From his peripheral vision, he saw her nose wrinkle.

"I bet you were a really cute kid. Like her," he nodded to the rearview. "How old were you when you learned to ride?"

"Five."

He could imagine her as a little girl, flying across the field on horseback. Found himself smiling.

"What did you like to do as a child?"

He was still half-disbelieving that she was making conversation with him at all.

"I drew."

"Hmm."

"What?" He dared a quick glance at her. She seemed thoughtful, her head leaned to one side, her eyes unfocused as she stared out the windshield.

"I just thought you'd say football or hockey or something."

"I played a little, but it wasn't my favorite thing. Until high school, when I realized—"

He cut himself off, but she'd always been good at reading him.

"Until you realized... you could get girls if you played sports?"

Heat crept up his neck, but he nodded. "My home life wasn't the best. The popularity of being on the basketball team was... nice."

He'd clung to those friends. Even as teenagers, they were more constant than his emotionally distant dad and enabler mom. When they'd offered him a place to spend weekends, it had been easy to go with the flow.

And when they'd introduced him to partying, he'd loved the oblivion. The ability to forget his life for a little while.

Only he'd hadn't realized it would have such far-reaching consequences.

Anna didn't pursue his comment about his past. Maybe she hesitated to get in too deep. Instead, she asked, "Are you missing the city?"

"Surprisingly... no." It was true. "I mean, I miss my bed —the hotel..."

She snorted as if she knew what he meant. It was old.

"But folks have been welcoming. It's kind of nice that when I stop for coffee, the gal remembers my name."

"Like that old sitcom theme song?" He could hear the smile in her voice.

"Something like that." He'd been empty for so long. Tried to make himself part of a community, find the family he craved, looking in all the wrong places.

When things went bad, party friends were the first ones to go. At least in his experience.

Somehow, even though he'd only been in Redbud Trails for ten days, it was starting to feel like home.

Especially when Anna slanted him a smile from across the cab.

His mouth went dry, and he wanted to blurt out something crazy—like asking her out on a date, but she pointed to a side street as they drove into town and he saw the sign for an auto parts store.

Saved by the destination.

ANNA HAD INSISTED on going into the auto parts store alone. Even though Kelly planned to help her install the battery, she could purchase one on her own.

She'd left Gina with him, and as she lugged the

weighty new battery out of the store, her eyes went to the pickup parked in the first spot.

Huh. She couldn't see their shadows inside the truck.

She drew closer and realized the windows were down, but no one was inside.

Heart pounding, she rounded the side of the truck and then stopped short.

There they were. Sitting on the lowered tailgate, legs dangling, talking quietly.

Eating ice cream.

She approached, and they were too busy watching the traffic passing on the street to notice her.

"When I grow up I'm gonna be a princess," Gina said.

Anna opened her mouth to forestall anything Kelly might say in response. Even at three and a half, Gina had a vivid imagination, and she didn't want him to squash her dreams, even if they were silly.

"Will you have a big, fluffy, pretty dress?" he asked.

"I'm gonna have a gazillion million of them. More than fit in my closet. And lotsa tiaras, too."

He pointed to her cone. It had started dripping chocolate down one side.

Gina slurped at it, and he winced a little.

Anna smiled. He obviously hadn't realized what a mess a little girl and an ice cream cone could make. He was probably imagining her getting in his truck all dripping with chocolate. Which wasn't far off.

"Will you live in a big castle?" Kelly asked.

"No, silly." Gina's words were exaggerated, as if Kelly

should know the answer. "I'll live on the farm with all my horses."

"Ah. I saw you riding with your mom the other day."

"I'm a good rider," Gina said proudly. "When I turn five, my mama's gonna buy me my own pony, and I'm gonna name it Philip."

She shook her head, even though they couldn't see her. Gina had asked about having her own pony since she could barely talk. Her first word was "mama" and the second was "horse." She'd become obsessed with getting her own pony named Philip—after the prince on one of her favorite animated movies.

Her arms started to ache from the heavy weight of the battery.

She shifted, and Kelly looked over his shoulder, eyes going wide.

He jumped down the moment he saw her, coming toward her. "Let me—"

But he still had a half of a melting cone in one hand, and attempted to juggle it to grab the battery. "Here, you take this—"

How?

"I've got it," she huffed, and moved to the place on the tailgate that he'd vacated. She shoved the battery over the edge and exhaled in relief. Flexed her fingers.

"How come the cashier didn't carry it out for you?" Annoyance colored his voice.

"He offered."

His eyes took her measure and he nodded. "And you said you'd do it yourself."

He didn't seem to be judging her for her independence, but his earlier teasing about asking for help still rankled. She didn't have a problem asking for help. When she needed it. Which wasn't often.

"You guys got ice cream without me?"

His eyes cut to her from the side. "I got you a strawberry milkshake. It's in the truck."

Her favorite. He'd remembered.

He turned to catch Gina before she jumped out of the pickup bed, leaving Anna to try and settle the butterflies swirling in her stomach.

His admission about his family from earlier had touched her. And now this kindness was a reminder that not everything had been bad between them.

They'd had a lot of fun together. More so before the date gone bad. And then the awful way he'd embarrassed her at her wedding reception to Ted.

She'd let that last vivid memory color her memories for far too long.

Maybe she was finally ready to let go.

CHAPTER 7

*A*nna crunched into a rainbow-colored snow cone as she watched Mikey and Gina play chase around the lawn in front of the church building after weeknight Bible classes.

Lila and Melody stood beside her, the humid air prompting Melody to lift her curls—dyed a cute shade of pink this week—off her neck.

"So the kitchen's shaping up?" Melody asked. "And just in time for your birthday."

"The cabinets look completely different with the darker stain. And the granite is..." She pretended a swoon as she crunched another bite. Kelly had surprised her by asking some of the men from the community to help. Brothers Maddox and Justin Michaels and their cousin Ryan had spent hours over several evenings working in her kitchen, and she almost thought it could be done by her birthday—her goal way back in the beginning when

83

she'd hired the contractor who had taken off with her deposit.

"Who cares about the construction," Lila said. "I want to know how the romance is shaping up."

"What?" Anna half-laughed the word even as her insides fluttered. "There's no romance."

"No romance?" Lila parroted. "He sat next to you at Sunday morning's worship service."

"And took you for ice cream in Weatherford," Melody added.

"That wasn't a date," she protested. "The battery on my truck was dead."

Her friends shared a look.

And suddenly Mikey was there. "Can I have a bite?"

Anna surrendered her snow cone to his noisy slurp.

"Thanks, Mom!" He pressed it back into her hands, but turned to walk backwards, facing her. "Don't forget, Kelly said we're leaving at five o'clock for the carnival on Friday."

She waved him off. Face going hot, she kept her focus on the treat in her hands.

Her friends remained silent, but she could feel their stares.

But she could wait them out.

She crunched through the rest of her snow cone, the cold in her mouth a counterpoint to the humid summer evening and the heat in her cheeks.

She finally reached the bottom and tossed the paper wrapper into a nearby trash receptacle. When she turned around, ready to gather up the kids to go home, she found herself blocked in by her friends, who now stood shoulder-to-shoulder with arms crossed and expectant expressions.

"Carnival?"

"Friday night?"

Her face warmed all over again.

"It's not a date. It can't be. The kids will be there."

And no one dated with their kids in tow, did they?

"What's wrong with it being a date?" Lila asked.

Melody's expression had softened. While Lila had spent her early years in Redbud Trails and recently returned, Melody had been here in those dark days immediately after Ted's death. She'd weathered some of the storm of grief with Anna.

"Honey, it's been almost three years," she said quietly. "Maybe it's time to think about dating. Being in a relationship again."

It seemed like that was the only thing she *could* think about since Kelly had come back into her life sixteen days ago.

She shook her head. "Even if I were thinking about it... not Kelly."

"Did you ever wonder if God brought him back into your life for a reason?"

She didn't want to think that. With their shared past, it hurt too much. She smiled tightly. "To reno my kitchen."

She couldn't continue with this conversation. "I've got to get the kids home and through the bath." Though she had a more lax bedtime during summer break, they still needed their rest.

But Lila and Melody's words ran through her head the entire way home as Mikey and Gina talked with each other about their respective Bible classes.

Maybe it's time.

God brought him back into your life for a reason.

She didn't want to think about Kelly taking Ted's place in her life. Ted had been steady. A rock that she could always count on. It had been easy, comfortable to love him.

Her feelings for Kelly had never been like that. They'd been thrilling ups and devastating downs.

He might seem more settled now that they were older —and now that he'd changed his life—but could she really trust that it would last?

SHE GOT the children in bed and took a cup of hot tea out to the back porch. Kelly had worked late with his extra helpers several nights over the last week and a half, but tonight she had the house to herself.

Kelly had asked her about the carnival—he'd seen a poster when they'd been in Weatherford—and Mikey had overheard and promptly dissolved into begging. How could she say no to that adorable face?

Now both he and Gina had been talking about nothing else for days and there was no way she could back out.

She hadn't wanted to think of it like a date, but after

Lila and Melody's words... Was that how Kelly saw it? Even with the kids tagging along?

She flipped on a sitcom but had a hard time paying attention as memories of their one and only official date swamped her.

Kelly had left her alone again.

She watched him heading for the wide red cooler that had taken two frat guys to carry over near the lone picnic table, which sat in the shadows thrown by the campfire. He stopped to talk to a couple of guys, and the three of them laughed uproariously.

Of the dozen girls and guys chatting, making out and chilling, she seemed to be the only one not having fun.

She'd been all in when he'd picked her up at her dorm room earlier. A bonfire had sounded romantic. Moonlight, another picnic with Kelly... maybe even a kiss goodnight.

She just hadn't planned on the party that several of Kelly's friends had brought with them.

Or for Kelly to drink so much beer.

She was a small town girl. A Christian, though she believed in living her faith more than shouting it from the rooftops.

She knew some of the kids in her graduating class of twenty-four spent the weekends drinking, but she'd never participated. Never really had the desire.

She'd tried not to mind when he'd had the first one. Tried to be cool about it. They were in college now. And he was older than she—he might already be twenty-one, though she wasn't sure.

But even if he were legal.., this wasn't exactly her ideal date, him spending the last two plus hours talking with his buddies and drinking.

And when he sat back down next to her—jostling her shoulder when he lost his balance—she could smell the alcohol on his breath. Maybe even coming out his pores. How many had he imbibed? Four? Six? More?

She stared at the fire, not looking at him. How was she going to get home? She refused to get in the car with him.

And from what she could tell, she might be the only one here who hadn't been drinking. So it wasn't exactly like she could ask someone else to drop her off at her dorm when they left.

Kelly bumped her shoulder again, but this time she knew he'd meant to do it. His current beer dangled from one hand between his bent knees.

"You wanna dance or somethin'?"

Someone had put the radio on in one of the cars nearby and turned up the volume, making it hard to talk. Several couples danced inappropriately.

"Maybe take a walk?" he went on when she didn't respond.

She turned her head to look at him. His eyes rested on her. They were too bright, a flush high on his cheeks. There was no way she was walking in the dark woods with someone she didn't know well, especially not when that someone was three sheets to the wind.

Now she had to question how deep their friendship really went.

She'd had a crush on him from the first day they'd met in Professor Dee's COMP II class. Been stunned when he'd struck up a conversation after class. And even more so when he'd sat next to her for every class period. They'd become friends easier than she'd ever dreamed possible. Her heart quickened every time they were together.

And when he'd asked her out, she'd been thrilled.

But now... she would never see him the same way again.

When she'd hoped for wooing and conversation, she'd gotten this instead.

"Anna?" he prompted when she still hadn't answered.

"You know, I've got a huge term paper for my sociology class," she said. He didn't have to know it wasn't due for several weeks. "I shouldn't stay out too late or I'll never be able to focus on it tomorrow."

Something dimmed in his eyes, but he smiled widely. Maybe a little too widely.

"All right."

Canned laughter brought her back to the present and the flickering screen against the darkness of her bedroom. After she'd appropriated his keys and driven him back to his on-campus apartment, Kelly had tried to kiss her. He'd missed, resulting in a sloppy open-mouthed kiss against her cheek. His hands had been everywhere. She'd been trapped between him and the truck.

It had been too much.

She'd shoved him away, ducked beneath his arm and rushed home.

The next time she'd seen him in class, he'd acted as if nothing had changed. But everything had.

She'd met Ted during her sophomore year, and though she and Kelly maintained something of a friendship, he'd slipped to the periphery of her life.

Until her wedding night, when he'd shown up at the reception—he hadn't been invited to the wedding—obviously drunk, and taken over the DJ's microphone. He'd shouted that she'd made a mistake, married the wrong guy as she and Ted had escaped under a shower of tossed rice—and curious glances.

Ted had been so angry. She hadn't had a defense for Kelly, but their friendship had always been a sore point for Ted, and they'd fought. On their wedding night.

Other than a friend in high school and Ted, she'd never dated anyone else.

Maybe she should call off the carnival event. The kids would be disappointed.

But there was also a part of her that wanted to be brave enough to explore what could be between them.

Could she really do it?

CHAPTER 8

*L*ate Friday afternoon, Kelly dunked his head beneath the outside faucet next to Anna's horse corral, sucking in a breath at the shock of cold.

It felt good after hustling and working a long stretch after his lunch break.

He'd been so close to finishing the backsplash between Anna's counter and upper cabinets that he hadn't wanted to go back to the hotel and change before taking Anna and the kids out. He'd rushed to get his tools locked away in the kitchen or the toolbox in his truck bed and then to wash up. Her birthday was tomorrow, and he'd worked overtime and beyond to finish the kitchen for her, knowing how badly she'd wanted it as a gift to herself.

He was thankful he had a clean T-shirt in his truck and a pair of tennis shoes to switch out for his work boots.

He worked as much of the tile glue as he could off his

hands before drying them and his face with a clean towel he'd also—amazingly—found in the truck. A horse blew nearby, but he didn't startle. He was getting used to the animals being around.

Getting used to the open spaces.

When he turned to reach for the dry T-shirt he'd hung over the fence, he spotted Anna, standing several yards away, staring at him.

Her eyes were locked on his bare chest, and suddenly self-conscious, he grabbed the shirt and pulled it over his head.

She cleared her throat, but still didn't speak. Her eyes remained on his now-covered chest.

Which sent a thrill of pride right through him.

"Sorry. I'm running a few minutes late," he said.

As if his words had snapped her attention, she averted her eyes. Brushed a strand of hair behind her ear. Blushed.

She was attracted to him.

He'd hoped. But until now he hadn't been sure.

And the last thing he wanted to do was trample her heart again.

But he couldn't wait for their night out.

"You ready?"

She kind of hummed and shrugged.

He dug in his pocket for his keys.

Mikey and Gina were hopping around his truck like two jumping beans, and the drive to the Weatherford fairgrounds was full of their excited chatter.

Even Anna had lowered her guard and talked about

the freelance marketing she did and some of her humorous clients.

This. Being here. Like they were a family.

This was what he'd been missing his whole life.

His heart was full.

Anna glanced at him, their gazes connecting. And she smiled a warm, open smile.

It gave him a high better than anything he'd ever experienced.

And made him brave enough to clasp her hand once they hit the fairgrounds and the noise and lights of the carnival surrounded them.

And she didn't pull away.

ANNA HAD no idea what she was doing.

Holding hands with Kelly like they were teenagers.

Letting him buy her cotton candy—which the kids immediately pilfered.

Mikey and Gina missed nothing. When they noticed her holding hands with Kelly, their faces lit up.

They were so bubbly and chatty that she had to wonder how she'd been holding them back by clinging to her quiet grief over Ted's passing.

It was time to move forward with their lives.

And for the first time, she could admit that maybe Kelly was a part of that.

The kids begged to go on rides, and when she protested going on the whirly tilting ride, even Kelly got in on the action, cajoling until she finally gave in.

On the ride, with Mikey at his side and Gina at hers, Anna found herself pressed against Kelly's muscular side.

And when he stretched his arm around her shoulders, sparks went off.

His rich laugh weaved warmth around her, and when he and Mikey swung the carriage in a crazy loop to Gina's delighted shrieks, she couldn't help laughing too.

He begged off when the kids demanded a ride on the Ferris Wheel. And of course she teased him about his fear of heights, but he refused to relent.

She allowed Mikey and Gina to ride together and stood just outside the barrier for the ride, watching. This time when Kelly clasped her hand, his fingers slid between hers in an intimate grasp.

She craned her neck up as Mikey and Gina's cart rose and rose, aware that Kelly was looking down at her.

"What are we doing?" she whispered.

She wasn't even sure he could hear her over the noise of voices and music from the carnival games and shouting vendors, but he answered, voice low too, as if the intimacy of their conversation demanded it.

"We're holding hands."

She swallowed hard. "Is that all?"

Mikey leaned out over the edge of the carriage, waving wildly. The perfect opportunity to break the contact with Kelly, but instead she lifted her opposite hand and returned the wave.

He squeezed her hand lightly. "It's a lot more than that. For me." His voice was sandpaper rough, and when their eyes met, he didn't hide the vulnerability in the depths of his gaze.

Her stomach swooped as if they were the ones on the ride.

"Is... that okay?" he asked.

Mikey and Gina shrieked as their carriage passed by, and she was relieved for the distraction of waving at them.

"Kelly, I..."

I'm scared.

He squeezed her hand again, gently. "You don't have to decide right now." He took a deep breath. "Being with you and the kids... well, they're amazing, and so are you."

Heat flared in her cheeks, and joy thrilled through her. Even so, she couldn't seem to catch her breath.

"I thought I might stay in Redbud Trails. Longer than for just your kitchen reno. I've got lots of folks asking me to work for them, and I'd like to see where this thing between us goes."

Face-to-face, looking up into his eyes, the bottom of her stomach dropped out.

Before she could answer, Mikey and Gina ran up, shouting over each other.

ANNA HADN'T RESPONDED to his declaration that he wanted a relationship. Not really.

Their time together was almost up. The kids had been a constant presence since they'd gotten off the Ferris Wheel and walked through the house of mirrors and then burned through fifty bucks playing games to try and win a stuffed animal for Gina. And he couldn't complain about the kids' presence, because he loved every second of their time together.

Mikey was funny and never could seem to finish his sentences fast enough. Gina was a doll, and her sense of wonder made him see things in a whole new way, things he normally took for granted.

Being around the three of them made Kelly feel... whole.

The punch of emotion was almost too much to bear, too painful in its fullness.

He loved them.

And he was in love with Anna. Still.

It had taken maybe a day for all his old feelings to rekindle. Seeing her take care of the kids—often sacrificing her own needs for theirs. Watching her entire being light up when she was with the horses.

Hearing her laugh. Receiving her smile.

But he was intensely aware that she hadn't said she wanted him to stay.

They turned onto the rutted dirt drive that wound through the front pasture of her property.

Mikey and Gina had dropped off to sleep, and the silence between him and Anna was too thick.

He brought the truck to a slow stop in the middle of the pasture and turned it off.

His headlights illuminated the twin tracks in front of them. The moon wasn't out, and stars were the only other light. The truck clicked as the engine cooled. Cicadas serenaded them.

"What are you doing?" Anna whispered.

He angled his body, leaning back against his door so he could see her. Blue light from the dash lit her face, but her eyes remained shadowed.

"Once we hit the house, you'll have your hands full getting those two into bed. Maybe we could talk for a little bit. Plus, it's nice out."

His palms were sweating.

And when Anna met his gaze steadily, his heart thundered in his ears.

"That's probably a good idea."

I love you. The words were on the back of his tongue. He wanted to say them so badly.

But there was a part of him that hesitated. Knew she might not be ready to hear it.

"You came to Redbud Trails to tell me something. Will you tell it to me now?"

Stunned into momentary silence, he tried to force air into his lungs.

She wanted his confession, *now*?

He'd settled into working on her kitchen and stealing whatever moments he could with her and her kids. He'd pushed the real reason he'd come here to the back of his mind.

Maybe there was a part of him that wished it never had to happen.

Was she bringing it up now to put distance between them? Because she was scared of her feelings for him?

Or—dare he hope—because she wanted to move forward with him?

"One of the steps of the recovery program I worked was to share my testimony with the group. If it's okay, I'll start with that."

He swallowed hard, not sure he was ready for this.

Would Anna look at him with disgust and turn away, as his father had?

Whatever happened, this moment would forever change their relationship.

He stared out the windshield into the dark pasture because it was easier than looking in her eyes.

"Your kids are really lucky," he started. "When I was growing up, I didn't have..." He gestured to the two sleeping kids in the back seat. "This."

And he'd wanted it so badly. Needed it.

"My parents were distant and sometimes, my dad lost his temper."

He stretched his arm along the back of her seat and stared out the windshield. After a moment, her hand settled on his, startling him.

She clasped his hand loosely, offering him comfort.

ANNA WATCHED Kelly's expression change, but the tight stretch of his lips wasn't his real smile, not the open and warm expression he gave her so often.

"It wasn't completely awful," he said. "Just..."

She heard what he didn't say. There were things from his childhood that hurt him.

"During my teen years, I got introduced to the party scene, and I started to feel like I belonged with them. When I got drunk, I could forget that my parents didn't seem to care about me. At least for a little while."

"How old were you?" she whispered.

He shrugged, his eyes far off, caught in the past. "I don't know. Fifteen. Sixteen?"

So young.

"By the time I got to college, it was more habit than anything. Sometimes I didn't come up for air for entire weekends. I was drinking every night."

He sounded disgusted with himself. "I told myself I could control it."

He breathed deeply, and she had to force an exhale, realizing she was holding her breath.

"Then I met you."

His eyes flicked quickly to her face and away. Her gut tightened, settling like a rock in her lower belly.

"I knew you were special from the first time I saw you."

His words hung between them, almost tangible.

She'd felt it too.

"I couldn't believe it when you actually talked to me—gave me the time of day. And then you agreed to go out with me."

She remembered—too well, probably.

"I was so nervous on our date," he admitted. "I thought one or two beers would take the edge off."

"But then you kept going back for more," she said softly.

She saw his Adam's apple bob as he swallowed.

"I could see myself ruining our date, but I couldn't stop it. It was like a car wreck, but in slow motion. I..."

He shook his head.

"You were right to shut me down," he went on. "You deserved someone who had their life together, like Ted."

He glanced at her, maybe unsure that he should've brought up her late husband. There was more. She could sense he wasn't done.

"Even after you started dating him, after I knew I'd blown my chance, I told myself I could quit anytime. Denial. Then you were getting *married* and... I went on a binge."

He blinked, and she saw the emotion moistening his eyes. "I ruined our friendship, made a scene at your wedding—"

She didn't tell him about the fight—couldn't. It was over, long over now.

"And I'm sorry. That's what I came to Redbud Trails to say. I know I don't deserve your forgiveness, but I want it."

The tone of desperation in his voice showed just how much.

"You have it," she whispered. It was easier than she'd expected.

His face crumpled, and he bowed his head. He breathed deeply, his shoulders shaking.

She didn't let go of his hand.

After long moments, he raised his opposite hand and scraped the heel of his hand over his eyes.

"Thank you." He finally said, and his voice was hoarse. "That means... a lot."

She smiled tremulously. She had to know. "Will you tell me about your recovery?"

He nodded. "I kept spiraling. I quit a couple of times, but it didn't last. And every time, the guilt would hit me hard. And it took more and more to find the oblivion I craved. My drinking started affecting my work. I was hungover half the time. Or drinking earlier and earlier in the day. Or... just drinking through."

She shivered, imagining him doing what he was doing now with less-than-perfect concentration. Those saws and other tools were dangerous. Not to mention moving heavy items or climbing ladders... Anything could have happened to him.

He smiled a small, rueful smile. "I know. It's a miracle I didn't get hurt."

"God must've been watching out for you."

His gaze lingered on hers, and he swallowed hard again. "I'd like to think so. No one else was. I'd cut off my parents by the time I was out of college. Cut contact with friends who might've tried to help me."

It seemed... lonely. She couldn't imagine coming back from Ted's death without her friends surrounding her.

He went on. "But the lowest point was the car accident. Of course I was DUI."

She squeezed his hand, suddenly afraid to hear what he was going to say.

"Thankfully, no one was hurt. It was a fender bender in broad daylight. But the cop really read me the riot act.

I don't know if he'd seen some bad DUIs or had a family member involved in one or something, but he was passionate about it. I spent the night in jail. Sick as a dog, hungover, scared. It wasn't my first offense. I was driving with a suspended license. The judge gave me two choices. Jail time or find a place to dry out. I chose to dry out."

She was so glad it hadn't been worse.

"My mentor in the center told me it wasn't going to stick unless I joined a long-term recovery program, and he was the one who hooked me up with a local church and the program there. I owe him everything."

She had to shake her head at that. "You owe him a lot, but you made the choice to change your life, and I know it wasn't easy."

"It's still hard sometimes. Coming here was hard. Facing you. Knowing you probably had plenty of disgust left for me." He took a deep breath. "When I tried to make amends with my dad, he threw me out of the house."

Oh, Kelly.

KELLY FELT as if a weight had been lifted.

Anna wasn't running away. She hadn't asked him to leave.

She was still holding his hand, and her eyes were shining up at him.

He needed her closer. "Do you mind—could I—?"

He reached for her and was gratified when she

scooted closer and came into his arms. He couldn't resist bending his head. He kissed her.

If holding Anna was like coming home, he didn't have words to express what kissing her was like.

Heaven, maybe.

When he pulled away, he was glad to see she was as out of breath as he was.

He pressed his chin against her temple, not ready to let go yet.

But eventually, she said, "I should get the kids in bed. Will you text me when you get back to the motel? So I know you're okay."

His chest swelled. She wanted to check up on him. "Sure."

He shifted to face forward again, turned on the truck and kicked it into gear with his left hand. No way he was letting go of her. He eased the truck into motion. He didn't hit the gas, just let it ride in slow motion.

"What are you doing?" she whispered.

"Trying to make the moment last." He'd take every second with her he could get.

As he'd meant her to, she smiled. He felt the change in her expression where her cheek was pressed into his shoulder.

But even with the slowest driving he'd ever done, they pulled up to her house before he was ready.

Maybe he'd never be ready to leave her again.

"Who—?"

She perked up, straightening in her seat and he

followed her gaze to where his high beams illuminated someone sitting hunched over on the front porch steps.

Tim.

"Gimme a minute," he said before opening his door and getting out of the truck. He left his door open, the dome light on.

What was the younger man doing here? Glancing around, Kelly didn't see another vehicle.

And then he got close enough to smell him.

The stench of alcohol was strong even from feet away.

Without even a hello for his friend, he returned to the truck to tell Anna to wait a few minutes before she got the kids out.

But she hadn't waited inside after all. She must've followed him out his door. In the pale starlight, he could see from her expression she'd realized Tim's condition.

CHAPTER 9

*A*nna's phone vibrated from her nightstand, the screen lighting up her dark bedroom.

She squinted against the brightness, peering at the screen.

12:30 am.

She hadn't been asleep.

When she didn't open the phone, the text message flashed again.

KELLY: *Sorry it's so late. I got back to the motel ok. Can't wait to see you in am.*

TEARS FILLED HER EYES, blurring her vision.

The screen went dark due to her inactivity.

She used the back of her hand to brush away the tears.

She needed to just rip off the bandaid. Being with Kelly tonight had been... perfect. Too perfect, maybe.

Seeing Tim, receiving Kelly's apologies as he'd helped load his inebriated friend into the cab of his truck, it had brought back too many memories.

Too many fears.

What if she did open herself up? Continue on in this relationship with Kelly?

And what if he fell off the wagon? Went back to his old habits?

She had to think about her kids. Had to protect them.

But it wasn't her kids she was thinking about now.

What if she fell in love with Kelly, and he left her? Either through choosing his old lifestyle again or by dying, like Ted had.

She'd barely survived losing Ted. Some days she still felt like half of herself was missing.

She didn't think she could risk loving someone again.

And that's what made her open her phone.

ANNA: I think we made a mistake tonight. I'm not ready for a relationship again.

HER THUMB HOVERED over the SEND button for a long moment. Could she lose him again, after coming so close.

Just one date?

So like last time.

She could still see Tim on her front step. Could smell him. If Kelly went that route...

She pushed SEND.

Seconds later, the phone rang in her palm. *Kelly.*

She should have known the stubborn man wouldn't let things go so easily.

She meant to hit the button to reject the call but must have missed through the blur of tears in her eyes, because the line opened up with a click.

She didn't say anything.

"Anna?" His voice was small through the connection, and she lifted the phone to her ear but remained silent.

"Honey, what's wrong?"

Everything.

She swallowed and tried to find the words to end things between them.

He exhaled heavily and when he spoke, his voice was rough. "Anna, if I rushed you with anything that happened tonight—that kiss—"

He broke off.

She said nothing.

He said, "I'm sorry if I rushed things."

He hadn't. She'd been right there with him. Maybe even falling in love.

But fear kept her silent.

"We can go as slow as you need to. Just keep working on our friendship and see what it grows into. I was thinking I could find a place—a real place—here in Redbud Trails. Sure seems like there's enough demand for a contractor or handyman—"

"No!"

The word burst from her.

If he stayed, she would see him everywhere. In a small town like Redbud Trails, there would be no avoiding him. And she didn't know if she could be that strong.

There was a long, expectant pause between them.

He cleared his throat. "Tell me how to make things work between us, and I'll make it happen. Anything."

She closed her eyes against the sting of further tears. Bowed her head. Forced the words out.

"I had the life I wanted before Ted died. What we had was... comfortable. Safe. But now everything is different. With you... I can't." Her voice broke on the last word, and she covered her nose and mouth with the hand not holding her phone, trying to mask the sound of her tears.

"Don't cry, honey." That was fine for him to say, but she would swear his voice was wet with tears too. "It's okay. Everything's going to be okay."

But if life had taught her anything, it was that rarely did things turn out *okay*.

KELLY LUGGED his battery-powered drill case to the bed of his truck and secured it in the tool compartment. He started winding the hose from his air compressor.

Sweat rolled down his back and dampened the hair at his nape. The late afternoon sun beat down, baking the earth all around, so he tried to stay in the triangle of shade made by the porch roof and his pickup.

He'd asked Maddox and Justin Michaels to round up

some guys and finish the touch-ups for Anna's kitchen while they'd been at the carnival in Weatherford. He hadn't asked her permission for the guys to be there while the house was empty, but he trusted them.

And they'd done a great job, leaving him only a few final touches today, like installing the stainless steel stove and dishwater he'd bought her.

If he'd hoped for a chance to talk to her in person, change her mind after their late-night phone call, it'd dissipated like ice melting in the hot summer sun when he'd seen her this morning. She'd been pale, her eyes red-rimmed and shadowed.

Obviously the decision she'd made hadn't been easy on her.

There was a part of him that wanted to rail at her. Demand she give him a chance. Beg her some more, even after he'd embarrassed himself on the phone last night.

But the bigger part of him understood.

He would never be able to shake the shadows of his past. He'd made those choices, been a slave to his addiction for too long.

And if she couldn't live with that, maybe it was better to find out now.

He could never measure up to Ted. And he knew it.

He tossed the coil of tubing into the bed of the truck and went back for one more look at the newly minted kitchen.

He'd wanted her to be surprised to find it done today —her birthday. And his other surprise was yet to come. Soon.

She'd avoided the area all day.

He'd been so down that he'd called his sponsor at lunchtime, had a good heart-to-heart with his mentor, a man who'd been there and could understand Kelly's broken heart. He'd also checked up on Tim, who'd been sober and serious. Kelly encouraged him to visit the recovery program that had helped him work out his issues, but he didn't know if the younger man would really do it. And it had to be his choice.

Now he ran his fingers along the gleaming countertop and moved to take down the plastic he'd hung in the doorway that first day.

He backed toward the outer door as he folded it.

His time here was up.

He'd gotten what he came for. Anna's forgiveness, even though he couldn't have her.

And he'd given her this gift.

It would have to be enough.

The doorbell rang as his boots hit the back porch, and he gently closed the door.

Being shut outside didn't stop him from hearing Mikey's pounding footsteps or Gina's shout as they vied for answering the front door. His heart thumped painfully. He would miss those two almost as much as he would miss Anna.

He stowed the plastic in the compartment and then reached for the end of the long orange power cord snaking its way across the back porch. It was the last thing to clean up.

Multiple voices came from inside, and with the

kitchen window on this same side of the house, he saw silhouettes as bodies moved through the kitchen he'd just vacated.

Her party had arrived.

He knew she'd wanted a party to celebrate her birthday with her new and improved kitchen, but he also knew she hadn't thought it would be finished in time, not after the first contractor had stolen her deposit.

And he'd wanted to give it to her.

He'd spent all week coordinating things with her friends Lila and Melody via text message, and now the night was here.

And he was stuck on the outside.

He stowed the heavy coil of power cord and locked the compartment down, then moved to the tailgate to shut it.

Somewhere along the way, he glanced up at the window again, and there she was, looking out at him.

He gripped the closed tailgate with both hands, fighting against the desire to rush inside and declare everything he felt for her.

He loved her.

If he thought there was any chance it would be enough, he would've done it.

But with his father's voice ringing in his ears—*get out of my house!*—and Anna's tearful *I can't* from last night still echoing, he forced one hand to release the tailgate and give a casual wave before rounding the pickup and getting in.

He was done here.

CHAPTER 10

*H*e'd really gone.

Anna had allowed the distraction of the surprise party—where each guest had arrived with food or drinks—and admiring her new kitchen last night, but when dawn broke the next morning, she found herself wide awake. And doubting herself.

Had she made a mistake?

Tell me what to do. Anything.

What kind of man renovated a kitchen—all the way to purchasing new appliances—without expecting payment? Or planned a surprise birthday party for a woman he hadn't seen in almost a decade?

Someone amazing.

She wasn't on the verge of falling for him. She'd fallen.

But she was still afraid to risk her heart.

She tiptoed outside, running one hand along the gleaming countertop as she passed through the kitchen.

She cared for the horses, then turned them out in the corral.

When she got back to the house, she found Mikey was the first one up, which was unusual. Maybe he was just excited about visiting the Oklahoma City water park, as she'd promised him and Gina.

They'd been planning it since school had let out for the summer.

But when Gina still didn't wake a half hour later, Anna went to check on her and found her feverish and complaining of a sore throat.

The trip was off.

After she'd plied Gina with children's Tylenol and juice, she found Mikey sulking in the new kitchen.

"I'm sorry we can't go today," she said. "I promise another time, okay?"

He shrugged and looked at the back door.

"What's wrong?"

"When's Mr. Kelly coming back?"

"He's not." She wanted to reach out and put her arm around him, but the almost-nine-year-old wore a defiant tilt to his chin, and his eyes sparked angrily.

"He promised he'd build a tree house with me."

She reached out and ruffled his hair. The small contact would have to do. "I'm sorry, honey."

He shook her off. "It's not fair! Kelly promised!"

He slammed out the back door, and she didn't even have the heart to reprimand him.

Through the window, she watched him run out to the barn.

HE WAS SUPPOSED to be leaving Redbud Trails in the dust, but Kelly made his way down the familiar dirt road toward Anna's. Maybe for the last time. He'd made a promise, after all.

He slowed his truck as he neared the spot where Anna's fence had been knocked down before.

Something was wrong.

Heart suddenly thudding and adrenaline surging, he let his eyes rove in an arc. Threw the truck into park.

The fence was down again. A large cow with danger-ous-looking horns was standing on the opposite side of the road from the break in the fence. It's head was lowered, and it swung those horns side-to-side.

And then Kelly saw Mikey, standing a few feet outside the break in the fence.

His hair was mussed, his shirt ripped across the middle, as if he'd already been in a tussle.

The cow bellowed and galvanized Kelly into action. He threw open the door and yelled for Mikey. His shout hadn't been necessary. The boy was already headed toward him.

From the corner of his eye, he saw a blur of motion as the cow charged them.

Kelly grabbed Mikey around the middle as the boy neared, then whirled back toward the truck.

Not fast enough.

He tossed Mikey into the cab but couldn't get in before the cow's shoulder rammed into the door, slamming it closed behind Mikey. Probably left a dent. Had the boy gotten out of the way, inside the truck, in time?

Sharp pain knifed through the back of Kelly's right shoulder, and he spun wildly against the side of the truck.

He could feel the animal's hot breath on his back and knew that those dangerous horns were *right there.*

He got one of his steel-toed boots on the back tire and launched himself up and over the truck bed.

He tripped on the two-by-fours piled in the back and went sprawling, but didn't roll out thanks to the lip on the other side.

Afraid that the cow would somehow be able to climb in on top of him, he scrambled for purchase and lifted one arm to wrap around his head.

Then he heard a shout and a strange buzzing sound.

He waited for the cow to butt into the truck again. For the feel of its hot breath.

When nothing happened, he gingerly raised his head.

Anna was there, on horseback, wielding an electrified wand as she put herself between the cow and the truck.

"Get on!" she yelled again, and the cow ambled for the fence.

When it had crossed the fence line—totally unconcerned as it wandered back on to Anna's property—she kicked one leg over the horse's back and whirled for the door.

Kelly hopped the side of the truck bed as he heard her tremulous, "Mikey?"

He moved up behind Anna as the boy launched into

her arms, sending her staggering back. Kelly steadied her with a hand to her lower back but quickly moved away as soon as she'd found her feet.

"Are you hurt?" Her desperate fear was audible in her voice, and Kelly saw her turn Mikey's head in her hands, run her hands down his arms, looking for injury.

"Mom, I'm all right. I'm okay." Mikey's voice was strong and clear, and relief sent Kelly staggering. He clutched the side of the truck with one hand.

"What happened?" she demanded, still looking Mikey over.

Mikey sent a sheepish glance toward Kelly.

"I was riding Samson bareback, and he threw me and ran off. I was walking home and didn't see the bull in the pasture. When I did, I tried to duck through the fence, but he found that hole and started chasing me. Then Mr. Kelly drove up and saved me."

He'd been so very lucky to have arrived in time, to have realized what was going on in time to shove Mikey into the cab of the truck.

Anna turned to him, and the tears sparkling on her cheeks were a punch in the gut.

"You're bleeding." She looked a bit stunned as the words escaped her mouth.

He looked down and sure enough, the shoulder of his T-shirt was ripped, and blood ran down the back of his arm.

"Let me see." She was shaking as she grasped his elbow in one hand and used the other to peel back his sleeve.

He craned his neck to see the damage.

Blood seeped from a deep scratch in the meaty part of the top of his shoulder.

Anna gasped slightly.

"You hurt, Mr. Kelly?" Mikey stepped closer, and Kelly put his uninjured hand to the boy's shoulder, keeping him in front.

"It's not bad. Dumb thing ruined my favorite T-shirt, though."

Anna's eyes were a little wild as she turned toward the cab. "You cleaned your truck out," she accused him.

She moved around him and went to the horse, touching the saddle and then making a strangled sound of annoyance.

"I don't have anything to staunch the blood." Her voice was shaking, her movements still erratic.

And Kelly couldn't take it any longer.

When she passed by him again, moving back toward the truck, he took both her elbows in his hands.

"Anna. Anna." He squeezed her slightly until her eyes focused on his face. "We're okay. Mikey's okay. And so am I."

She was still shaking.

"Take a breath."

She sucked in a deep inhale and shocked him when she launched herself at him, throwing her arms around his neck.

He buried his face in her hair, letting the last vestiges of fear and adrenaline drain from him. Movement came from his side, and then Mikey burrowed into his side. Kelly let his arm come around the boy's shoulder.

Even if Anna couldn't love him, Mikey was safe.

For once, he'd been in the right place. Done the right thing.

Anna eased away from him, and he let her go, emptiness rattling his chest as she went.

She brushed at the tears on her face. "Let's go get Gina from the house—she was sleeping when I ran out after Mikey—and I'll drive you to the doctor's office. You might need stitches."

"It's not that bad," he said quietly. "If you've got a butterfly bandage, I'll fix it up myself."

Still a little shaky, she nodded. "All right. Can you drive?"

"Yeah."

"Then come up to the house." She picked up the horse's reins, motioning for Mikey to follow her.

She settled into the saddle and pulled Mikey up behind her.

He waited until she'd cleared the fence and loped off back toward the house before he put the truck in gear.

ANNA COULDN'T STOP SHAKING, even after she'd run up to Gina's room to check on the still-sleeping toddler and settled Mikey in the living room with a book.

The boy wanted to recount Kelly's rescue over and over, but the images were already playing in a loop in her mind. Kelly shoving Mikey into the cab of his truck, then being spun around by the bull.

If he hadn't been able to get up, if he hadn't had the strength to vault into the truck, the bull could have easily trampled him or caught him more fully with its horns.

She dialed an old friend even as she ducked into the hall bathroom for the first aid kit.

"I need to sell the bull," she said after they'd exchanged greetings.

She found the red plastic box beneath the sink and stood up, bringing it with her.

"It's about time," came the response.

She couldn't deny it. She'd put it off for too long, and look what had almost happened. "Can you pick him today?"

Through the window, she saw Kelly's pickup parked near the porch.

She ended the call and opened the back door. Kelly hesitated at the bottom of the porch steps, hands shoved in his pockets. The flow of blood had slowed from his shoulder, but the sleeve of his T-shirt was darkened with an ugly red stain.

He caught sight of her, and his eyes cut away. There was none of the ease, the warmth in his expression that there had been just two days ago, before she'd reconstructed her defenses against him.

"I was thinking I could just drive back to town and the motel. I'm sure I can find some supplies at the pharmacy and then I don't have to—you don't have to—"

He was trying to let her off the hook.

She opened the door further. "Get in here."

He brushed his good hand through his hair. Exhaled through his nose.

And then followed her inside.

"Take off your shirt," she said.

He complied, looking around and then tossing it out the back door. Conscientious. Not wanting to get her new kitchen dirty, though she wouldn't have minded. Not when he'd saved her boy.

"Sit down."

She kicked a chair out from the nook table and brought the first aid kit over as he settled in the seat.

She placed a hand on his shoulder. "I should have sold that bull last year, when he started showing violent tendencies. And I should've made sure the fence was fixed. Asked for help."

He looked over his shoulder at her, and their eyes met and held.

She leaned down and kissed his cheek.

"Thank you," she whispered. "For being here. For saving Mikey."

He nodded. Swallowed. "I'm just glad I was there."

She grabbed a washcloth from a drawer and doused it in warm water from the faucet. Back at the table, she sponged away the blood caking Kelly's arm.

"Why were you driving out here?" she asked idly, because the tension coiling in her stomach threatened to erupt.

He didn't answer. She angled herself at his side, and

being there gave her a view of his cheeks as color rose high in his face.

She kept wiping his arm, finally taking his hand in hers. "Hmm?" she prompted when he remained silent.

"You weren't supposed to be home," he muttered.

He'd been coming *here*?

She'd seen the stack of two-by-fours in the back of his truck. But the kitchen was completed. What then...?

It came to her in a rush. She liberally applied antibiotic ointment to his scrape and then stuck the largest bandage she had on it.

He watched her with his neck craned back, and when she'd finished securing the bandage, he stood up.

"Thanks for patching me up." He rubbed the back of his neck.

"You came to build Mikey's treehouse."

"You were supposed to be at the water park," he said. His eyes were anguished.

"You're still gonna build me my treehouse?"

Mikey darted into the room. He must've been eavesdropping in the dining room.

Kelly dropped one hand on Mikey's head and fished in his front jeans pocket with the other, coming up with several sheets of notebook paper. He laid four flat on the table. The first was an almost-perfect copy of the sketch Mikey had shown him. The second was of the underside of the structure, showing support beams. The third and fourth showed details of the interior from two angles.

"If it's okay with your mom, I think we can finish it today."

Mikey looked up at him with equal parts shock and hope. "You want me to help?"

"It's your treehouse, isn't it?" But the pleading glance he cut to Anna said differently.

He'd planned to be here when they were gone, out of deference for Anna.

She kept her eyes on Kelly as she said, "Mikey, honey, can you go check on Gina for me? Don't wake her up, just peek into her room."

"Aw, mom..."

"I need to talk to Kelly."

Her son sighed loudly, making no effort to hide his annoyance. She squeezed his shoulders, blinking back images of how easily she could have lost him. "Thank you."

When he'd gone, the tension rose between her and Kelly, and she couldn't hold his gaze. She moved to where her hip brushed the corner of the table and allowed her fingers to trace the edge of one of the sketches. "I can't believe you did this."

He remained silent. Maybe he was waiting for her to kick him out. Or say her piece and then kick him out.

She gathered her tattered courage and looked up to find him watching her.

"I think... I made a mistake."

His eyes shadowed. He ducked his head. "The kiss?"

"No."

His head jerked up.

She took a step toward him, her hand gripping the back of one of the kitchen chairs. Swallowed back her fear. "When Ted died, I thought a part of me died with him. The only thing that kept me going was knowing the kids needed me."

Compassion lit his eyes.

Maybe she swayed toward him, or maybe he moved toward her, but suddenly the gap between them had narrowed.

"It's taken a long time for me to come back to life. And when you showed up on my doorstep, it was like waking up. Or maybe like when your arm or leg goes numb and then wakes up and you feel pinpricks of sensation. It hurt... at first."

She was babbling like Mikey.

She lifted her chin and met his eyes squarely. "And then, it scared me. Remembering just how lost I was when Ted died... I didn't think I could be strong enough to do that a second time. It felt like too big of a risk."

He seemed to understand the past tense of her statement, because his hands rubbed up behind her wrists, up her arms and rested behind her elbows, pulling her in close.

She let her hands settle at his waist.

He brushed a kiss against her temple. "And now?"

Her hands flexed against him. "After this morning..." She didn't know how to explain what she realized. It all seemed so silly now. "There's risk everywhere."

She leaned forward, and her chin brushed his chest. Shuddered, thinking about what could have happened to the both of them.

"Now that I'm awake again, I can't go back to sleep," she whispered.

One of his hands cupped the back of her head tenderly. "I wish I could be a sure bet for you," he murmured. "With all the junk in my past... All I can do is try every day to prove to you that I'm a different man than I was before."

She tipped her head back so they were face-to-face, so close. "I'm falling in love with the man you are now."

Intense emotion flooded his eyes, and he squeezed them shut, leaning his forehead against hers.

His breath warmed her lips, and then he opened his eyes, examining every inch of her face. "I..."

He couldn't seem to find words, but he kissed her temple, her cheek, her nose and forehead. Then he claimed her mouth.

For the first time since he'd come back into her life, she let herself go in the kiss, let emotion—love—roll over her in a crashing wave.

And while the fear was still there, it didn't engulf her.

Kelly broke the kiss, tucking her close to his chest. "I love you, Anna. I think I've been in love with you since the day I met you, but back then I didn't know what it really meant."

He kissed the top of her head. "If you want to go slow, we'll go slow. I can drive up from the city once a week..."

She tilted her head back again. "Maybe not *that* slow..."

The joy shining from his eyes was unmistakeable, and it connected with a matching joy deep within her.

Kelly leaned in and brushed her lips with his.

"Mom! Are you kissing Mr. Kelly?"

She broke from Kelly's embrace, but not too far, because she wrapped one arm around his waist.

Mikey's expression was hopeful and half-ornery.

"You think it would be all right if I started seeing more of your mom?"

Mikey's head bobbed in an enthusiastic nod. He came further into the kitchen, and Anna reached out to ruffle his hair. "You two had better get to work on that tree-house before it gets too hot outside. I'll call you when it's time to come in for lunch."

Mikey ran out the back door, boots slapping against the new tiled floor.

Kelly followed her son but threw one last glance over his shoulder, one just as full of hope and joy as Mikey's had been.

EPILOGUE

146 DAYS LATER

*A*nna watched as Kelly and Mikey passed the football, racing down the field. Several boys from Mikey's third grade class, along with their dads, had coordinated the impromptu no-tackle game.

She held Gina on her lap, soaking up possibly the last nice autumn day. Though the sun was out, the November air had a definite bite to it.

"Whoo-hoo!"

"Go Mikey!"

The dual shouts from behind her heralded Lila and Melody's presence as they flopped down on the blanket beside her.

"Lila!" Gina abandoned Anna's lap to throw herself at Lila, who caught her with a laugh.

"What are you guys doing here?" Anna caught sight of

the blue streak in Melody's hair and raised her eyebrows, but her friend just shrugged with an enigmatic smile.

"We saw your car and thought we'd stop and see what you were up to," Melody said. "You've been spending all your time with Kelly."

"I have not." Anna playfully nudged her friend's shoulder. They'd had a girls' night earlier in the week and driven to Weatherford for manicures and a late dinner, then chatted until far too late in the night.

Mikey ran by with a "hey, mom!" and Anna whistled loudly and clapped.

"Who is *that*?" Lila asked, her eyes on one of the players jogging across the field.

Melody openly gaped. "He's *fine*."

"His name is Weston Moore. He's a prodigal, like you, Lila."

Anna remembered him well from high school. He'd been on the fringe. Not someone she'd hung around with. He'd had a reputation for recklessness, especially with girls' hearts.

He'd been wild.

A little bit like Lila, who was now contemplating Melody's ongoing narrow-eyed stare of the handsome blond.

Weston would be much better suited to Lila and her flare for adventure.

But there was still one thing Lila hadn't faced.

"Have you been out to the ranch yet?" Anna asked, drawing both Melody and Lila's attention. Lila's expression went from open and laughing to pinched and closed off in less than a heartbeat.

"I guess that's a *no*."

Since Lila's return to town seven months ago, she'd been avoiding returning to her family's ranch. Her mom and dad had passed away, and the ranch continued working under the management of foreman Ben Taylor. He'd been after Lila since before she'd returned home to come out to the property and make some hard decisions about what to do with it.

Anna had known Lila back in elementary school, before Lila had gone away, but she didn't know the mystery of why her close-mouthed friend didn't want to go home.

Before she could push for more details—or revisit Melody's interest in Weston—Kelly rushed off of the makeshift football field and collapsed on the edge of the blanket. Conveniently, his head fell in Anna's lap.

"I'm too old for this," he gasped, pushing his sweaty fringe of bangs off his forehead. "Your son is running circles around me."

Refusing to be ignored, Gina abandoned Lila and jumped onto Kelly's stomach, making him double up with an "oomph!" before he commenced tickling her.

"Get off of me, you heathens," Anna said with a laugh, pushing at his sweaty shoulders.

But Kelly and Gina just gave each other a long look and then tickled Anna as her friends scooted out of the danger zone.

When she'd subdued them with a squirt from Mikey's

water bottle, she pushed her now-tangled hair out of her eyes and shook her head. "Never go after the mama bear," she said, mock-seriously even as she pointed the water bottle at Kelly.

His eyes promised retribution for later, but the corners of his mouth pulled in a smile.

The football players dispersed, and Gina ran off toward Mikey, leaving Anna and Kelly shoulder-to-shoulder on the blanket with Lila and Melody angled beside them.

"So..." Lila said with a leading pause. "We're dying to know how serious you guys are."

Anna's face went hot, but not because of the question.

"We know you started out taking things slow," Melody added. "But it's been months. Are you guys going to tie the knot or what?"

She felt the instant tension in Kelly, but she didn't dare look up at him. Since the day he'd declared his feelings for her, he'd been careful not to push too fast. She'd been planning to talk to him about this very subject—tonight, in fact—but not in front of her friends. She sent a glare their way, then thought better of it.

After all, they'd started it all when they'd pushed her to accept his help with the kitchen.

Why not give them what they wanted?

She cocked her head up at the man who'd changed her life since he'd come back into it. "Well...?"

He looked down to her, his eyebrows shooting up to his hairline. "Well, what?"

"We have been moving pretty slowly. What do you think about taking it up a notch?"

His eyes narrowed slightly as his hand settled on hers on the blanket between them. "What exactly are you saying?"

She ignored the giggles and whispers from her friends behind her. It wasn't easy. "I'm saying I think we should get married. Not today. But... soon." She hadn't told him yet, but the small claims court had judged in her favor against her former contractor, and she had socked the money away for a wedding.

Something lit deep in his eyes. Like he was afraid to grab onto the hope she was giving him. "Are you sure?"

Nerves bubbled in her stomach. "Are *you* sure?" she returned.

Now his eyes had a spark of another kind. He stood and pulled her to her feet. "Honey, I've been sure since the day you got me up on that horse for the first time. Sure enough to carry this around." He slipped a hand into his jeans pocket and came up with a small black drawstring bag. He opened it and dumped a sparkling diamond ring into his opposite palm.

"Well, then we're both sure." But that didn't stop her hand from trembling as he placed the solitaire on her finger and lifted her hand to kiss her palm.

"They're both sure," Lila stage-whispered.

Melody's words were a gibberish squeal that drew Mikey and Gina, who started dancing and shouting until the whole park knew their news.

In the middle of all the commotion, Kelly spun her in

a wild circle, his deep laugh reverberating through them both.

He finally set her down, touching his forehead to hers. "I love you."

"I love you, too," she returned.

He lowered his head to kiss her, his lips smiling against hers at Mikey's "aw, not *again*."

"You'd better get used to it," Lila muttered.

ALSO BY LACY WILLIAMS

WILD WYOMING HEART SERIES (HISTORICAL
ROMANCE)

Marrying Miss Marshal

Counterfeit Cowboy

Cowboy's Pride

Courted by the Cowboy

TRIPLE H BRIDES SERIES (CONTEMPORARY
ROMANCE)

Kissing Kelsey

Courting Carrie

Stealing Sarah

Keeping Kayla

COWBOY FAIRYTALES SERIES (CONTEMPORARY
ROMANCE)

Once Upon a Cowboy

Cowboy Charming

The Toad Prince

The Beastly Princess

The Lost Princess